Other books written by KEN BUMPUS:

"Those Crazy Camera Guys"
(A fact/fiction novel of the adventures of a Navy
Combat Camera Group in Vietnam)
ISBN # 978-1-4669-0623-5

"Navy Photographers In Vietnam"
(Sequel to above listed book following a second
Navy photo team)
ISBN # 974-1-4669-3006-3

"American Made"
(Author's Autobiography)
ISBN # 978-1-4669-9374-7

"King of Devil's Canyon"
(The tale of a wild horse wrangler in the early west)
ISBN # 978-1-4907-4734-7

All published by:
Trafford Publishing

>www.Trafford.com<
888-232-4444

Available on-line at Barnes & Noble, Amazon and
most of your favorite book seller (on order)

PI Inc.

(A Fictional Novel About a Chicago Cop
Turned Miami Private Investigator)

Ken Bumpus

Trafford rev. 09/18/2015

Trafford PUBLISHING® www.trafford.com
North America & international
toll-free: 1 888 232 4444 (USA & Canada)
fax: 812 355 4082

ONE

The room was dimly-lit and quiet but for the hum of the various mechanical apparatuses that surrounded him.

"Where in the Hell am I"?
- The figure on the bed mentally inquired to no one in particular.

His only conscious sensation was of a warm sponge slowly moving over his forehead and neck.

He attempted to open his eyes but with little success. A slight lift of one heavy eyebrow and still all he could perceive was the foggy image of someone's face leaning over him.

"Well, Detective, you're finally back with us," a soft voice whispered into his consciousness.

"wmmf wmy?" he attempted to speak but the tubes entering his nostrils and mouth prevented any coherent sound coming forth.

"Take it easy, there, Sweetie" the soft whisper continued. *"You've been out of it for a while. You have to*

1

stay still while I finish this sponge-bath. I finished the embarrassing areas while you were asleep so I'll only be a minute or two more. You just keep quiet, it'll be a few days before you can start asking questions,"

Detective Third-grade Patrick Ireland was recovering from several gun-shot wounds suffered when he got caught in the cross-fire between two rival street gangs. He was still alive thanks to that pesky vest he was forced to wear. Five bullets from an AK- 47 assault rifle had caught him off-guard.

Two of the shots had caught him in the upper thigh, two had been stopped by the vest and the single shot that almost cost him his life, entered through the vest's arm-pit gap and penetrated his left lung.

In and out of consciousness, 24/7 of touch and go, his life was hanging by a thread. He lay in a medically-induced coma and was kept under close observation by Dr. Clyde Moore, the thoracic Surgeon who had removed the near-fatal bullet.

The gun-shot wounds to his upper thigh had shattered the bone and steel rods now held his leg together. It was feared he might lose the leg or, at least, be hobbled for life.

HA!!! The doctors hadn't counted on Patrick's strong constitution and determination to become whole again. Working diligently with doctors and therapists, Pat's will to recover from his life-threatening wounds slowly won out. Six weeks into his rehab and physical therapy, he was able to put some weight on his injured leg and at the end of four months, with the aid of a cane, he was walking on his own albeit slowly and a little shaky.

His mission, which led to him sustaining the several high-caliber wounds, were the result of an operation to quell gang war-fare in South Chicago. He was leading a force of ten heavily armed street cops and a five-man SWAT team, sent to break up a 'turf war' between two of Chicago's deadliest street gangs. This latest skirmish was where Detective Ireland found himself caught in their cross-fire and sustained his wounds. Rival street-gangs continue to plague Chicago's South side with robberies, rapes, drug dealing and any <u>thing illegal under the sun.</u>

The Chicago Police Commissioner had promised the citizens :

"These young hoods cannot hold the city hostage. We're going to break their hold and bring crime in Chicago under control," he declared.

"Besides enforcement the City is instituting several various training and sports programs to funnel their energies into more peaceful activities.

"The shooting of Detective Ireland HAS to be **the last casualty** in our battle for the youth of the City of Chicago!"

This latest skirmish brought to a screeching halt the stellar career of Chicago's ace Detective, Patrick Ireland. Despite the miraculous recovery from his wounds the Review Board decided to put him on permanent, 100% disability. **He was being '*Put out to pasture*'!**

Now, Patrick was going to have to decide what to do with the rest of his life. Friends suggest writing a book about his many police-related adventures, but he kept putting that off. He couldn't imagine parking himself at a desk, punching words into a computer. Too dull!

Relief came when he received an e-mail from one of his former police department partners. Ex-Captain Ian L'Rosa had retired two years previously and now lived what he told Patrick was the "greatest life of leisure in the world"

"The beaches, the fishing and the climate are ideal," he laid it on to convince Pat to move to Florida.

He was juist getting used to being "EX-Detective Ireland" and was seriously considering Captain L'Rosa's suggestion of retirement in Florida.

The Captain's last point - The climate turned the corner for Pat when one of Chicago's infamous early-winter storms blew in off the lake and the cold caused the scars on his leg wound to ache.

Twenty four hours of enduring the freezing wind off Lake Michigan and Patrick Ireland was on the phone booking a flight to Miami.

In an e-mail to Captain L'Rosa he told him of his plan.

*"Cap, **I'm on my way!** I'll be there on the 6:20 Southwest tonight. Book me a hotel room and we'll apartment-hunt tomorrow. Something where I can see the ocean. You know the area and can steer me to finding my new 'digs'. Hope you don't mind the short notice, but I needed a nudge to help me decide to make the move.*

*"**Yesterday's Arctic Blow was all I needed.!***
See ya, Pal."

Patrick was apprehensive about leaving Chicago behind but he had no one there to hold him back. Flo, his wife of 20 years, had been taken by cancer two years ago and his grown twin sons both lived on the west coast. They had their families and couldn't visit him except on rare special occasions. Besides, travel from Oregon to Miami wasn't much further than from Oregon to Chicago.

The shock of going from the frigid Lake Michigan cold into the balmy 74° Miami sunshine made Pat struggle to shake off the shock to his system.

"Hey there, Irishman," Pat was welcomed by Captain L'Rosa as he was retrieving his two pieces of luggage from the carousel

"Hey yourself, you old Wop! Look at you! Bermuda shorts, flowered shirt and flip-flops. And that bronze tan and sun-bleached hair (what there is left of it)! You really look the part of a transplanted Chicago South-Sider," Patrick shot back.

"I've got room for you at my place, so forget these over-priced hotels. My apartment has two bedrooms and Sally is off visiting our daughter and her family in Missouri so there's plenty of space!"

"Sounds great," Patrick replied, "but I want to get an early start in the morning looking for my own 'digs'."

"Well, Pat old chum, I just may have the answer to that problem, too.

"When I got your e-mail I contacted the Real Estate agent Sally and I dealt with for our place. I figured she might have something that would fit in your budget. As it turned out she no longer handles rentals - - but - she was asked by one of here former clients to unload her condo for her.

"The condo had been purchased through Ellen's agency four years ago. The couple was quite well-to-do and bought it to join the many 'Snowbirds' in their yearly migration (that's the name given to rich folks who can afford a home up north for six months summer-living and a second place down here to spend six months away from the cold winters up north)".

Ian went on "Two months ago the husband suffered a massive coronary and the widow decided to stay in Connecticut near her family and sell the condo. It sounds like it's just what you need - 1600 square feet, one bedroom, a den, living room, kitchen and all that other stuff that makes an apartment a home.'

"All well and good, Pal, but that doesn't sound cheap; What's the 'vig'?"

"That's the sweet thing about it. Ellen has worked out a deal with the widow to offer it on a lease with option to buy contract. All the owner wants is enough to cover her taxes and condo management assessment fees, plus 20%. As I said, this is a **sweet deal'**. You came along at just the right time."

Bright and early next morning the two were off to meet with Ellen and see just how 'lucky' Pat was.

The building's an eight-year old 20-story high-rise sitting along the Intracoastal Waterway in north Miami.

"It was constructed post hurricane 'Charlie', which veered north from Cuba and headed up the Florida coast, spreading devastation all along the Atlantic," Ian informed Pat, "New construction laws in effect after the storm mean the building is about as safe from hurricane damage as is possible."

"That's nice to know, Cap,"

Ellen was waiting for them in the lobby and greeted them with a sparkling smile.

"Hi, Captain, long time no see. How's that beautiful wife of your's? ---Sally isn't it?"

"Yeah. She's doing great. She's visiting our daughter for a couple weeks. I understand you've moved up a notch in the real estate business."

"Right. I made some excellent contacts and now only handle high-end estates. Seven figures and up. What I'm about to show you is the last medium income property I'll be promoting.

"I wouldn't have this to offer except I'm handling it for a friend. She's one of the influential contacts that boosted me into the upper brackets.

"Come on, the apartment is on the seventh floor. The building has eight elevators so there's no stairs to climb. The roof has a lap-size pool and exercise room where the residents can keep fit or lazy around in the sunshine if they don't feel like the beach. Which, incidentally, you have a balcony that faces the east and provides a beautiful view of the Atlantic. From the roof-top you can also see the Intracoastal Waterway to the west."

"Man, I could really go for this, myself," Ian commented, "if Sally and I didn't already have a comfortable place.!"

As Ellen unlocks the door and swings it wide, she announces:

"Welcome to 'Riverside Towers', gentlemen!"

"Wow!" was all Patrick could say.

"All the furnishings you see will stay. The widow says the stuff holds too many memories. All she took with her were personal items. Even the linens are barely used. So, if you decide to take it, the apartment is ready for you to move right in."

"Break out the paper-work and show me where to sign!" Patrick exclaimed.

He wasn't kidding. They closed the deal in minutes.

He picked up his gear at Ian's apartment and settled into his new home. Within walking distance of his new home were numerous cafes and restaurants, bars and night clubs as well as two or three well stocked markets. His first stop after dumping his suitcases was to stock up his larder with the necessary items to sustain him, including beer and wine!

By four in the afternoon he was all settled in and, with some crackers and a glass of Rhine Castle he parked himself on his balcony to soak in the beauty of his 'front yard'.

"Ill have to get me a telescope so I can enjoy people-watching on the beach and admire the fancy boats cruising by on the Waterway." he thought to himself.

TWO

Waking up in the morning, he realized he hadn't closed the balcony drapes and discovered why it's called the Sunshine State The yellow sun with purple-red overtones was streaming into his bedroom with such intensity as to make further sleep impossible!

With sleep out of the question he performed his usual morning 'toilet'. He shaved and showered that's when he discovered what he hadn't noticed during his tour of the apartment the day before <u>luxury didn't end at the bathroom door!</u> Standing in royal welcome was a <u>walk-in tub with dozens of massaging jets.</u>

"If this isn't Heaven, it'll sure do 'til the real thing comes along!" he muttered to himself.

Patrick spent almost an hour in the tub, soaking and messaging his injured leg.

He picked up his cel phone and dialed Ian's number. After three rings Ian picket up.

"And a beautiful Florida 'Good Morning' to you, Irish" was his cheery salutation, "How was your first night in 'Paradise', Yankee?"

"Cap, I don't think you noticed yesterday, either but this morning I discovered that I have a **'walk-in'**

9

bathtub! Talk about living the 'Life of Riley' even he didn't have it this good!"

"You lucky dog, you!" Ian laughed, "That'll sure be good therapy for that gimp leg of yours. Next you're going to tell me you're going to run the marathon!"

"After an hour with those jets vigorously kneading my muscles I feel that's not such a far-fetched possibility! You got to come over and try it!"

"Don't tempt me or you're liable to have me knocking on your door before you hang up," Ian joked.

'No, Man, I mean it. You're welcome to come over and try it any time you need a boost. Right now I think I'm going to park out on my balcony and enjoy a glass of wine, some Wheat Thins™ and observe the oil soaked bodies on the beach."

"OK, you hedonistic Irishman. Watch out for that sun, though. It only takes a few minutes to cook that lily-white skin to a rare rosey glow"

"Warning noted, Cap. And, if I haven't said it before THANK YOU!

"Be seein' ya."

Pat was spending his retirement days lounging on his balcony, exploring the roof-top facilities, and taking long leisurely strolls along the beach. He tried a brief swim in the ocean but didn't care too much for the salty water. He decided he'd confine his swimming to the pool on the roof.

Soaking in the jets of his tub and an occasional workout in the exercise room, were quickly getting his injured leg back to normal functioning.

"By George, at this rate, I may surprise Ian and run the mini-marathon in the spring," Patrick mused.

The variety of different restaurants, Pat discovered on his walks, provided him with his choice of several different ethnic repasts. Chinese he was familiar with, but, in an adventurous mood, he had sampled the menus of Brazilian Churrascaria (pit-BBQ), Indian Curry, Turkish Shish kebab, and all sorts of other strange new treats.

His standby was of course PIZZA! He found a small family-run Italian restaurant just steps from the condo, which made the best pizza Pat had ever sampled. This became his favorite stop when returning from one of his strolls. He always ordered an "extra large with everything" taking three quarters of it home to snack on during the day, along with a chilled glass of Chianti.

Yeah, this was retirement at it's BEST!

In the following weeks Ex-Captain L'Rosa made occasional visits to check on Pat and sit on the balcony with him and enjoy a beer which he preferred over wine.

"Some Italian you are, NOT LIKING WINE!" Pat scolded, "I make a point of stocking Chianti, Rhine Castle and some of California and New York State's finest, and you sit here sucking on a bottle of 'Bud'!"

"I didn't drink anything stronger than 'Coke' until I began stopping off at the 'watering holes' with you beer guzzlers. I had been on the force five years before I starting liking a frosty glass of the 'brew'! Some positive example you guys set!"

"Each to his own poison, I say," Pat chuckled. "Have some more pizza, Cap. Can't let it go stale."

Patrick had never tried his hand at cooking, but, with all the appliances standing in his kitchen, he made an effort to put them to use. Ian was a gourmet cook and started coaching Pat in the niceties of simple food preparation.

"Cap, this is a whole new side to you I never imagined. This will save me splurging my meager savings on all these restaurants. That doesn't mean I'm giving up Papa Antonio's pizza, though! Even you can't equal the delicious pizzas <u>he</u> turns out!".

Patrick's retirement continued is this idyllic manner week after week. He was getting so 'laid back' he began to get restless.

"Cap, I've been sittin' on my butt, beach-walking, staring at the beach-bunnies and, in general, just plain being lazy. I need to find something to occupy my time!"

"I've been thinking the same thing, Pal. I've noticed you perusing the classified ads, looking at jobs and businesses for sale, so I did some enquiring around, myself, and I think I've found just what you need.

"Another ex-cop I know has a private investigation business in Miami which he's looking to liquidate or unload. He's been offered a very lucrative position as head of security in one of those Silicon Valley start-ups on the coast. He tells me they've offered him a salary that's almost criminal and he 'couldn't refuse'.

"The nice thing about this deal is he's willing to let his business go for peanuts. All his case files, computer, printers, software and furniture, to take up right where he's left off. In other words, 'lock-stock-and barrel'. He also says he'll throw in 'Sandy', his office manager-receptionist who knows all there is to know about P I 'n work. She also speaks 'Miami Spanish', which is essential to doing business in this town."

"When and where can I meet this P I? The idea intrigues me."

'I had a hunch you might be interested. You're more than qualified and, with the help of Sandy, it'll be a cake-walk. According to Andy, the cases are steady but not overwhelming. I'll give him a call and set up a meet."

The following day Ian showed up at Pat's condo and drove him to the office of Andy Jackson, the P I.

"Captain L'Rosa has laid out your background and, if you're physically up to it, I'm sure you could work out fine," Jackson assured Patrick.

"This business is a lot of phone calls, some computer savvy, lots of patience during surveillance and not much physical effort.

"Speaking of surveillance, if you're interested, for an extra two thousand I'll let you have my three-year-old van. It's a plain-looking vehicle on the outside, but I've customized the inside with just about all you'd need for a 'stake-out'. It's even got a computer and printer right there which comes in handy when you take photos of the subject. You can down-load and have high-quality pictures to hand to the client in 20 minutes. That's the beauty of digital technology,"

"Man, you got that right! I'll take it!"

"Then I guess all that's left is to do the paper shuffling. After that you can go down to the Court House and get your P I license. They'll want to see your Retired Police ID and I think you're set. I'll have the janitor scrape my name off the door and you can 'hang your shingle'."

"I've been thinking on that, Cap. I think I'll just put my initials on the door. Parrick Ireland **P I, inc.** he said with a grin. Fits, huh?"

"Now ain't you the clever one?" Ian guffawed

Their negotions were interrupted by the opening of the outer-office door.

"I'm ho-o-o-me!"

"That would be Sandy," Andy announced, "IN HERE, Darlin'. I have some life-changing news for you.

"Meet ex-Chicago cops Ian L' Rosa and Pat Ireland. Pat and I have just put our 'John-Henrys' on a sales contract and he is now the new owner of this agency."

"Well, this is news! I knew you were toying with the idea of taking that job on the Coast but this comes as a huge surprise!" Sandy choked.

"Glad to meet you, Sandy," Patrick said, "Andy tells me you're the heart and soul of this business. Not to worry. If you're agreeable, I'd like to keep you on here. I'll need all the help that I can get becoming a P I,. Being a badge totin' cop and a private investigator are two different bags.

Sandy acknowledged the introductions and managed to smile through the shocking announcement.

"Of course I'll stick around, if you like. A job is hard to come by nowadays especially one you enjoy doing!"

"It's settled, then," Pat replied.

Besides being a business asset to the office, Sandy wasn't hard to look at, either. She was obviously Hispanic, with dark-auburn, shoulder-length hair, a light olive complexion and brown eyes that were intense and at the same time sparkled with hidden humor.

Yep, 'not a bit hard to look at'!

"For your information my full name is 'Alejandra Maria Sanchez de Torrez', but only 'Sandy' is acceptable. I'm third generation, USA born and raised, and damn proud of it. I served four years as an MP in the Marines and used my training there to get into the P I business. I'm single, unattached and liking it.

"Anything else you need to know will come as we get to know each other better."

"I think that should suffice for the time being," Pat laughed,

"I don't know what Andy's been payin' you but, if it's not enough, we can discus a raise down the line. I like to work with happy people. Now, do you have any questions?"

"No, but we have one open case that Andy had just accepted and had started a preliminary computer 'People Search'. I think we ought to get busy on that one as soon as you get settled."

"Sandy, I like the way you think. I have to get licensed today and I'll see you in the AM.

Patrick decided he would try out his new van and drove himself to the Clerk of Court's office and, with very little difficulty, had his P I license and headed back to his condo.

Andy's alterations to the van included a GPS direction finder so he set in the address and let the car tell him how to get home.

"Gads, I love this new technology," he marveled.

Sandy was already at the office when Patrick arrived next morning, and she handed him a freshly brewed cup of coffee as he walked in the door.

"I didn't know what you take in your coffee or if you like it black. It's my own blend of Cuban/Columbian so you'll have to fix it the way you like it."

"Thanks, I find this service to be confounding, But I can get used to it real easy,"

"Sugar, cream and a pint of brandy are over there by the sink, so help yourself. On your desk, I've laid out the files of all the cases we handled this past month with the unsolved one on the right. I have a phone call to make and then we can sit down and I'll guide you through them."

The morning went by rapidly with case file after case file being studied and discussed. Sandy was extremely organized and by noon they were finished with the completed cases and were ready to move on to examining the status of the one open investigation.

"That's enough for now, Gal," Pat remarked, "time for a lunch break. Care to join me?"

"I would but I have a meeting with one of my informants to see if he's uncovered anything new for me on a 'skip-trace' that's on our to-do list," Sandy demurred.

"Andy didn't tell me you do a lot of the 'leg-work' on these cases, but keep me in the loop if you find out anything interesting, will ya'?"

"Of course. Incidentally, I'm a certified and licensed investigator so I can join in on a case when needed. We're a team you in the lead and me covering your back," Sandy replied with a smile.

THREE

For the next several weeks, Detective Ireland was parked in front of his computer, getting an education from Sandy and Andy Jackson, who had agreed to delay his departure to the coast, to get Pat started on the right foot.

During one of Ian's frequent visit's to Patrick's place, he and Pat were enjoying their usual 'gab fest' on Pat's balcony when the talk turned to the Pat's P I venture.

"Cap, Andy is a computer **genius!'** Pat commented, "he's a self-taught 'GEEK'. He designed much of the equipment and software he uses in his work.

"He holds several patents and copyrights on his creations that's what caught the attention of that new Silicon Valley company," Pat continued, "They're buying temporary use and limited marketing of those inventions and offered Andy a couple hundred thousand bucks and that high-paying job to get him on their team."

"I recently heard something about his computer prowess during discussions I've had with friends in the local 'cop-shops'," Ian answered. "You really fell into a sweet deal, taking over Andy's operation."

"Thanks to you, Cap."

"Hey, Irish, you've just been lucky to be in the right place at the right time! With that four-leaf-clover luck you've had with the condo deal and the P I agency, you should buy a fist-full of 'Lotto' ticket!" Ian laughed, "Talk about 'falling in s..... t' and coming out smelling like roses', you GOT IT!"

"Buying 'Lottery' tickets might not be a bad idea!" Patrick said, tongue-in-cheek.

"You know, Cap, Andy has a GPS device another of his gimmicks about the size of a two-bit piece, which he uses when tracking and surveilling a subject. Of course, he has a lawyer who clears the way by getting a court-order before he uses it. It's illegal without the order.

"He's leaving all his proprietary apparatuses here on a loan/lease basis. I had to sign several non-disclosure papers to keep his inventions safe. So I have many investigative capabilities even most local cop houses don't possess," Pat marveled.

"He even has software for fingerprint (AFIS) and facial recognition that rivals the stuff we only recently acquired in Chicago.

"Sandy has been tutoring me in the use of all this paraphernalia. I don't know what I'd do without her help. She's a sharp cookie, another stroke of good luck!"

"I still suggest you try the 'Lottery'," Ian joked.

"So much for my P I endeavor. How about a slice of Antonio's pizza and a glass of wine. I mean, a 'Bud'?"

"Sounds good to me,!"

"The morning's early, so plenty time to lay back and enjoy the weather and **the view**. I notice the bikinis are out in force, so there's plenty diversion while we munch on the pizza," commented Pat with a leer and a chuckle.

"Lech! You better not let my jealous wife, Sally, find out how we spend my visits!"

"From the pictures of her I've seen all over your apartment, I don't think she has anything to worry about. She's as well equipped as any of those oiled-up bikini babes down there no insult intended!"

"None taken, Pal. And I agree. She's a 'dish'!"

"Four weeks of indoctrinating Patrick into the workings of a Private Investigating agency, and Andy had to leave for his new position on the Coast.

"Andy, I sure want to thank you for your time trying to get me started, here," Pat told him, "I'm certain, with Sandy having my back, we'll weather any sort of case thrown our way."

"I've tried to show you everything, but, if you have any problems, feel free to call me," was Andy's reassuring reply. "Good luck and good hunting!"

The first case **P I, inc**. was called on to investigate came with phone call from a Miami insurance company. There was an urgency to this case, so it was given priority.

Sandy took the call.

"We presently are paying a considerable figure every month to a claimant receiving disability for injuries on the job," the insurance rep told Sandy.

"He was working for a roofing company we were providing insurance for, when a ladder collapsed and he shattered his right rotator-cuff. He received a stainless steel replacement but his arm is allegedly paralyzed. It's a condition that's easily faked.

"We've received anonymous information that he may be scamming us and we would like you to check it out."

At Sandy's suggestion a 'face-to-face' was in order.

"Would three o'clock this afternoon be convenient?" she asked.

"I'll clear my calendar and have all our files on this guy ready when you get here," the insurance adjuster replied,

"The sooner we clear this up the better. We're so deep into this guy already, we have to know the truth before we throw any more bucks his way.!"

Patrick and Sandy arrived at the insurance agency offices and they were ushered into a conference room where, spread out on the table, were all the files including the doctor's report and the original background check on the suspect.

"You understand that we'll only be involved in investigating the pro-or-con of a case of fraud," Patrick reassured the two insurance executives at the table, "Any funds you'll recover are up to you. We're strictly investigators. we're not a collection agency."

"We're fully aware of that, Detective Ireland, Detective Jackson has done work for us before, and we're looking forward to renewing that relationship with you as the new head of **P I, inc**.

"Our records are all laid out here. We'll make copies of anything you'll need in your investigation. Our staff has been instructed to give you full cooperation."

"Fine. At present, our hourly rates are the same, so we'll sign the agreement and I'll get to work. You'll be getting a daily report as the case progresses."

'Good. And Sandy, glad to see your staying on. I'm looking forward to continuing to work with the Agency."

Returning to the office Sandy and Patrick discussed the next steps to take in setting up their search and surveillance of the alleged fraud subject.

"I'm going to hop in the 'Spy-Mobile' and take a ride over to the address this supposed-faker has listed on his dossier and scout out the area," Pat informed Sandy, "Care to go for a ride?"

"Thanks, but not today too much to do around here, right now," Sandy replied, "I do want to run over there soon, though, in case I might catch some of the surveillance duty."

"OK, hold down the fort and I'll try not to be gone too log."

"Buena suerte, Amigo." Sandy said "That means 'Good Luck, Friend' in Gringo talk."

According to the insurance records his target lived in a duplex on the west side of Miami in a town called Carlton City. With the GPS cranked up, He was able to hit the location on the nose. Finding the duplex was just as easy, so he spent the better part of an hour cruising the blocks surrounding it.

Across the divided boulevard from the duplex was a strip-mall where Pat decided he could park the van and, unobserved, set up his spotter position.

"This ought to be a 'piece of cake'," he thought to himself.

The day was still young so, for another hour, he watched the house. But there was no sign of his subject. When it grew dark, with no sign, Pat returned to the office vowing to be back in position before sun-up.

"I'm going to pack a lunch and a Thermos™ of you're strong coffee and spend the whole day parked on his doorstep," Patrick informed Sandy, "if he makes a move I'm gonna' get it on camera!"

A good night's rest, and true to his word, with the rising sun painting the eastern sky in pinks and purples, Pat parked the van in the strip-mall lot and settled into position with binoculars and video camera at hand, ready to roll.

The morning rush hour traffic was beginning to build but still no sign of the suspect.

At about eight-thirty Pat's attention was brought to full alert by the sighting of his 'target' emerging from his house with a small dog on a leash. The man's right arm was encased in a brace and all seemed normal. Pat emerged from the van and strolled down the boulevard parallel to the dog-walkers' path, watching intently for any unusual movement. The man and his dog returned home and entered the duplex.

Pat was just getting comfortable in his converted office chair when he was startled to see the man exit the house, minus the dog, and climb into his ten-year old pickup.

He backed out of the driveway and headed towards downtown. Pat's heart jumped in excitement to note the vehicle was a 'stick-shift' and the driver had no difficulty slipping his brace and shifting gears with his <u>right hand</u>.

"By Golly, I got you on tape, you crooked bastard!" Pat shouted under his breath, *"You screwed up once, you dumb **s. . . t**, and I'll catch you again and that'll be bye-bye disability pension!"*

Watching for the rest of the day produced no more sightings, so, as darkness fell, Pat cranked up his 'Spy-Mobile' and returned to the office.

Sandy was elated to hear of the day's success.

"At this rate we'll be wrapping up case number 01489 before the week's gone!" she joyfully remarked.

The second day of the stake-out produced only one sighting of the subject when he took his dog for it's daily stroll. Other than that, he remained in his house the remainder of the day.

On day three Pat observed him taking off in his pickup and heading for down-town Miami, the 'Spy Mobile' following at a discrete distance.

When he arrived at a strip-mall in southwest Miami, the pickup pulled in and parked in front of a chain steak-house. Pat noted that when he left the truck, he had shucked the shoulder brace.

"Aha,!" Pat thought, *"Let's see what you're up to, now, sucker!"*

Pat waited a few minutes before entering, not wanting to blow his cover.

He scouted out his target as he took a stool at the bar. From his position he had a clear view of the man's table. From his pocket he produced a tiny Hi-def video camera. It was very unobtrusive, about the size of a pack Marlboros. in fact it was painted to resemble the cigarette label. This was another of Andy's electronic marvels. Who could tell, even close up, what this gadget could do.

His steak dinner arrived and the suspect began to vigorously carve away at the piece of meat using his right hand to hold the knife!

"Gotcha, again you slob," Patrick silently gloated, *"This should convince any jury what a fake you are!"*

Pat finished his lime-soda, pocketed the camera and walked out of the restaurant, trying not to strut.

He arrived back at the office and announced his entry with a "WHOOP!"

"What the heck was that all about?" Sandy asked, "You scared the beans out of me."

"Just couldn't hold it in, Doll! Today should wind up case # 01489. I got video that'll sink that crook's money ship, for sure. I'll help you draw up our final report and charge sheet and I can deliver them to the insurance agent, first thing in the morning.

"As soon as we finish the paperwork I'm heading for my balcony to lay back with a chilled glass of Rhine Castle and unwind. Care to 'tilt one' with me no strings attached?"

"It sounds divine, Boss, but I'll take a 'rain-check'. Other previous plans."

"Well, I hope your 'plans' allow for relaxing. You deserve it!"

The insurance agency rep was overjoyed with **PI inc.'s** quick resolving of the high-dollar problem.

"I haven't looked at your charge sheet yet, but whatever it is, you'll find a bonus tacked on for the efficient way you came through for us!"

Patrick wasn't kidding as soon as he stepped into his condo he shed his street clothes and changed into Bermuda shorts, a tank-top, and bare feet and retired to his balcony, With his wine, some cheddar cheese, and a box of wheat crackers, on a tray, he proceeded to enjoy the Florida afternoon.

FOUR

Sandy was already hard at work on the computer when Patrick walked into the office.

"Hey, 'Little Miss Early Bird'!" Pat laughingly greeted her, "What'cha cooking up?"

"I just thought I'd pick up where Andy left of on this 'infidelity case'," Sandy answered.

"If you've got a minute, how's about filling me in."

"OK. This 'money-bags' woman thinks her husband has a 'sweetie' on the side and wants us to dig for evidence to use in a divorce. She's the one with all the assets and she wants to make sure he can't break their pre-nup and clean her out.

"So far Andy had discovered the guy's got two addresses one here in Miami and, records with the company he works for, show him living in Tampa.

He works as a traveling wholesale representative for a paper and stationary manufacturer so logs a lot of travel miles. His wife says he's out of town about seventy percent of the time.

"'Absence makes the heart grow fonder for someone else' I guess," Sandy joked.

"It happens," Pat agreed.

"I'll start doing some snooping around his workplace," Pat continued, "and see what his fellow workers might spill. Meanwhile, you stay on that computer. Those things have more secrets to reveal than a small-town gossip."

"Gotcha', Boss."

Pat spent about an hour snooping around the manufacturer's office and warehouse asking discrete questions. Apparently, though, the suspected philanderer was very closed-mouth and no one could shed a glimmer of light on his personal life.

"Sandy, I have his Tampa address and I'm going to hop a shuttle flight over there and do some detecting at that end of the puzzle.

"This bird has two nests and, somewhere therein lies the answer to this case, and I'm going to find it."

The flight landed eighty minutes later. Patrick rented a vehicle and headed for his next locality of the investigation. Without the GPS in his 'Spy Mobile' Pat had to rely on the age-old AAA paper map. The frequent stops to study the bungle-some folds took up a lot of his time so it was afternoon by the time he located the apartment listed in the case-file.

He called Sandy to inform her of his circumstances.

"Gal, I've barely scratched the surface over here so I'm checking into the 'Days Inn'™ on US 92 and getting an early start in the dawn's early."

"Understood. I haven't turned up anything earth shaking on this end so I guess we just 'keep keeping' on'."

"Right!" Pat answered, "See ya when I see ya."

Pat decided to try the direct approach in this case. He noted that the 'husband' had left the house earlier, so he walked up and knocked on the door.

An attractive 35 ± year-old blonde opened the door a crack and peered out at Patrick.

"Wha'dya want. If you're sellin' I ain't buyin' Make it quick 'cause I got stuff on the stove!" she greeted him.

"I'm not selling anything, Misses Ormond. Is your husband Clyde home?"

"Naw. He left this morning on one of his sellin' trips. Won't be back for two or three days. Anything I can do for ya?"

"I guess I should have called ahead. He's got some money due him and I just thought I'd drop it by for him. I'll catch him in a few days."

"You could leave it, I'll see that he get's it. How much is it for?"." she perked up".

'I'd like to leave it. It'd save me another trip, The check is for only $250 dollars, but he has to sign for it.," Pat replied, "Thanks for your time Ma'm. Have a good day."

And Pat returned to his rental car, got in, and drove away, leaving behind a bewildered woman still standing in the half-opened doorway.

"That ought to stir the pot and get something moving," He thought, *"She obviously believes they're married."*

Pat drove to the Hillsborough County Court House and checked the marriage records there.

"This guy sure isn't too bright in hiding his little 'love-nest'," He chuckled. *"He's even using his real name. I guess he figures the counties are so far apart, no one would notice.*

"He might have been able to pull it off, too, if he hadn't left his cel-phone lying around for his 'Miami wife' to find. Things like strange phone numbers, strange addresses and pictures, aren't always hidden in cyber-space. They sure tipped his play this time!"

Back at his motel, Patrick entered all his notes on his computer and called Sandy.

"Sandy, Partner, I have enough dope on this bigamist to sink him in Divorce Court, so I'm gonna' check in my rental and catch the afternoon shuttle flight home. See you 'on the flip-flop."

"I'll be glad to see you. That insurance guy we did the disability case for, has referred a couple of simple cases our way. I say 'simple' 'cause they look to me to be 'slam-dunk' jobs involving mainly computer searches."

On his arrival back in Miami, Patrick went directly to his office and, with Sandy doing the typing, made short work of smoothing out his bigamy case report

"Would you believe it, Gal, this dumb-ass was juggling a family on each coast for three years without either wife, his friends or his fellow-employees gettin' wise? Talk about asking for trouble!"

"Of course you know we have to turn copies of our report over to both Tampa and Miami PD. Bigamy is illegal in Florida and they may want to press charges," Sandy remarked.

"We're in the clear on this one, since we uncovered the evidence of a crime in the course of a 'civil' investigation," She reminded Pat.

"Yeah, but I feel good that we saved our client a bundle by diggin' this rat out of his hole!"

All the reports and charge sheets completed, Patrick said:

"Sandy, I'm takin' the week-end off for some 'R & R'. Then we can start fresh on those two pending cases Monday morning. You need time to unwind, too, so hit the beach or whatever relaxes you and I'll see you after the week-end!"

Friday, Saturday and Sunday Patrick turned off his phone and stretched out on his balcony. With a frosty glass of Rhine Castle and a couple of National Geographic magazines, he zonked out to read and study the roasting humanity on the white-sand beach below.

Sunday afternoon his repose was interrupted by an urgent pounding on his door.

"Now, just who in blazes can that be, messing up my 'day of rest'?" He grumbled and went to open the door before the pounder knocked it down.

"Why in Hell aren't you answering your phone," Ian asked in an irritated voice, "I haven't heard from you in a couple weeks and got concerned. I pictured you getting' caught spyin' on some philandering husband and winding up in the hospital or, worse yet, dead!"

"Sorry 'bout that, Cap. I've been keeping busy on the cases I inherited from Andy. Just decided to goof-off a couple days before putting my nose back to the grindstone. PI business is booming in South Florida," Pat apologized.

"Come on in here, I'm getting good use out of this balcony. Wanna' beer? I was just about to toss some of Antonio's pizza in the microwave. There's plenty. I stocked up before hibernating, so it's fresh!

"Bring it on, Irish, I can eat Antonio's anytime!"

Ian and Pat spent the afternoon 'shootin' the breeze', reminiscing about their Chicago days. Patrick proceeded to bring Ian up to date on his first days as a Private Investigator.

"I knew you'd fit right into being a 'Gum Shoe', old buddy," Ian remarked,

"Chicago lost the best detective they'd ever seen when you got taken out of their line-up!"

"Thanks, but, if not for you, I'd still be freezin' my gonads off up there. Just bumming around, living off my cop's retirement, sitting on a bar-stool in Clancy's with the gang and getting fatter by the day," Pat commented.

"It looks like that 'leg-shot' was a blessing in disguise when you get right down to it. It wasn't pleasant but, on analyzing it, I guess 'all's well that end's well'. Without that I wouldn't be living this 'life of Riley', swigging wine and watch the skin-show on the beach!" Patrick laughed.

"And having a new career as a PI and a lecherous old man!" Ian added, "Which reminds me, I'd best be getting home. Sally will be having a 'tizzy' I've been gone too long. Just had to check on you, though. Try to keep in touch in the future, huh, Pal?"

'Will-co, Cap."

Monday, Pat was at the office 'bright-eyed-and-bushy-tailed', ready to tackle another case.

"Boss, these two cases are both pretty routine so they shouldn't take too much 'leg work' to wind them up. The first one, #01489, I think I can clear up with a couple hours on the computer and a few phone calls.

"One of Miami's 'Little Havana' department stores is looking to hire a new junior, head-office executive and have asked us to do a complete background check on him. It'll most likely involve some Spanish exchange so, I would be the most likely one to conduct this investigation."

"As usual, you're right. Your linguistic prowess might come in handy, in this case," Patrick agreed, "Just one more reason I'm glad you stayed on."

"The other case is a bit more complicated, Boss," Sandy added. "One of Miami's larger real estate brokers has a customer bidding on a million dollar plus piece of property. They want an extensive financial report before they accept his offer."

"I can see why they'd want such a report. That's a pretty big bundle to be on the table," said Patrick.

"Sandy, what's the lowdown on the real estate buyer? Do we have contacts in the financial market that we can milk for information? It would be nice if we can 'touch base' there for the poop on this guy.

"I'll widen the search from there and make an in-depth financial background check. If this customer is all he claims to be, it should be a 'cake-walk', and we should be able to clear the case by the end of the week."

Sandy, true to form, had her employee background check wrapped up by early afternoon and a final report ready for their client by closing time.

Due to the complexity of case, # 01490, Pat was just getting a rolling start by day's end.

His first stop was at the buyer's bank, where he was able to ascertain that his subject did, indeed, have sufficient assets to cover his bid.

The following morning, Pat ran a credit check through all three bureaus and there discovered a slight discrepancy. Two of the credit card companies Pat searched, indicated that the subject had been running above normal balances in each of those accounts.

In spite of these unusual balances, the credit-to-debit ratio was not enough to squash the deal. So that's the report Patrick was able to turn in to the real estate client.

"Boss, I know, along with your certification, you were also issued a concealed weapon permit, but I never see you 'packing'," Sandy queried.

"Yeah, I have a 15shot Barretta clipped to my belt over my right hip. It's a retirement gift from the men in the precinct. Other than taking it out on the range to get the heft of it, I haven't fired a weapon since that night in Chicago, and I pray I'll never, EVER, have to fire it again!"

"Amen!"

The strident sound of the phone ringing in the outer office halted their interchange. Sandy picked it up and carried on a brief conversation before hanging up and moving into Patrick's office.

"Boss, that was Lawyer Endicott. He has a client that needs our help," she reported, "It's a touchy divorce case and he wants to come over and discuss the details."

"That's odd, but some of these divorce cases be can get kinda' 'Hinky'. What time did you set up for the meet?"

"We don't have anything on our calendar today, so I told him one p.m."

"OK, Wanna' grab some lunch with me? We can make it quick and be back before the 'sitdown'?"

"Thanks, but I brought a lunch. I'll just stick around the office and set of a 'casefile' so we can be ready for this one."

"See you in a jiff, then,"

Right on schedule Lawyer Endicott showed up with his client in-tow.

"Have a seat, would you like some coffee or bottled water?" Patrick offered.

"Thanks, but we'd like to get right to the problem, if you don't mind.

"I'd like you to meet my client Mr. Louis San Felipo. To get right to it Mr. San Felipo has a daughter who's engaged and he has some misgivings about the match. He wants a quiet background check on the prospective groom. If his daughter finds out her man is being investigated it will bring on the fireworks."

"No fear, sir. We'll handle your case with the utmost discression. Mr San Felipo, I'd like you to sit down in the other room with Sandy, here, and give her all the details.

"She speaks Spanish so, if you're more comfortable with Spanish, she can interview you in your native language. In whatever language, everything you tell her is confidential."

"Muchas gracias, Señor," Mr. San Felipo said.

"Mr. Endicott, we'll be back in touch with you and your client as soon as we have anything to report. If we don't run into any glitches, we should have results for you in 2 to 3 days."

As promised, after the search of several data-bases including the use of some of Andy's exclusive software, Sandy was able to give Señor San Felipo a favorable report on his future son-in-law.

"We ran the usual check, including traffic tickets, financials and social standings. In addition, we did do a thorough sweep of on-line social media for any questionable entries.

"Señor San Felipo, our findings show us a picture of an up-standing prospect for your daughter's marriage plans. Our best wishes to the couple and '*buen suerte*"(tr.: good luck) to you and your's.".

San Felipo, in gratitude for her work, included in his payment, an invitation to the wedding!

Patrick also rewarded Sandy with a gift card to one of the high-end restaurants for dinner for her and her man.

"Well done, 'Detective'!" Pat said as he hugged her, "Now enjoy a long week-end off."

Pat took his own advise and spent his weekend lounging on his balcony reading a detective novel, sipping Rhine Castle, and enjoying his panoramic view of the beach and the well oiled pulchritude basking in the warm Florida sun.

FIVE

BACK TO WORK

"Pat, your Chicago buddy, Ian, is on the phone,"
can you take it?"

"Sure, Sandy Hi, Cap, how ya' doin'?"

"Hi, yourself, Irish. I have to talk to you in private
if you can spare a few minutes. What I have can't be
discussed over the phne. How about I come over this
evening about 6 pm?"

"Yeah, that works for me. Meet me at my condo. I'll
order-in some pizza and we can munch and sip while
we talk.

Ian arrived at precisely at 6pm, accompanied by
another man, unfamiliar to Patrick.

"Pat, this here's a friend from 'Chi'. He needs your
services in a VERY confidential matter. I told him no
one else I knew could be more trusted than you! I'll let
him tell you his story, then you can decide if you want
to take his case."

"OK Shoot, Mr . . . ?"

"Let's just start by callin' me 'Mr. BUCKS'. As Ian has said, this is to be VERY hush-hush and I wish to keep my name off the records!

"To start with I was a very successful stock broker in Chicago but when Wall Street was 'on the skids' things got pretty 'hinky' in the investment world. My brokerage was clean but, when the FTC (Federal Trade Commission) started snoopin' around and asking questions, I realized the brush smears a 'wide swath' and can ruin even honest brokers' reputations.

"That's when I decided to 'cash-in', pick up my marbles, and quit the brokerage game.

"I survived the change and came out an extremely wealthy man. I bought a nice house on Key Biscayne and was enjoying the laid-back Florida life-style. I still did some investing on a personal level to keep my nest--egg liquid. In looking for a place to spend some of the accumulated 'loot' I came up with the idea of buying a boat and spending some of my life sailing the world."

"Sounds like an interesting plan, but where do my services come in?" Patrick asked.

"To repeat, this is all to be carried out on the 'QT'. I've located a real nice 85 ft motorsailor on the inter-net It's in a Ft Lauderdale marina and is priced so low I'm concerned about the legitimacy of the deal. Anyone can set up a website, and say anything they want about their business it doesn't have to be the truth!

"That's where you 'come in'. I've done all the background checking I can do BBB, the Inter-net and asking around the different marinas. So far no 'red flags' But their asking price is about 30% below market and I'm a bit apprehensive. It looks 'too good to be true'! I you know what I mean?"

"I do, indeed, know what you mean, 'Mr Bucks'." Pat replied.

"Before you step into this, Detective, I should warn you, from what I've uncovered so far, tells me the people involved have some very nefarious friends. I feel, if your investigations come to light, you could run into some violent reactions from those people. Can you handle that?"

"You're asking a former Chicago Cop? I can deal with any 'rough-stuff' comes my way!" Patrick chuckled.

"That's why I stress secrecy throughout this case. All I'm looking for is evidence that they're not trying to 'scam' me. I sure don't want anyone to get hurt in this deal!"

Shortly after sun-up Patrick was in his 'Spy Mobile' heading for Ft. Lauderdale. 'Mr. Bucks' had given him the address of the marina where the boat in question was berthed, but he decided he'd spend the day just wandering around the marina to get the 'lay' of the place, not paying attention to any boat in particular.

The marina contained about twenty berths with three standing empty so Pat took a leisurely stroll along the dock, stopping occasionally to study a few of the boats. Four of the boats had small 'For Sale' signs tacked on the dock's pilings. He paused at each of these to pretend to study the boats lines and overall condition.

He had spent the previous night studying the latest Yachting magazines to gain a smattering of 'know-how' so he could fake his boat-savvy, if accosted. He was careful not to show too much interest in the motor-sailor that 'Mr. Bucks' was interested in.

At noon Patrick scouted the nearest 'watering-hole' frequented by the boat people, and sat at the bar munching on a po'boy and sucking on a 'Bud'.

It wasn't hard for Pat to strike up a conversation. with the bar-tender and when he mentioned he was looking to buy a boat "if he could find one in his price range." the bartender called one of his other customers over and made introductions.

"Soapie," he said, "this here is Hal (Pat's undercover name). He's shopping for a boat. You know any good craft for sale in the $80 to $90 K price range?"

"Well, there ain't anything like that right here, but I hear Captain Ramos has something on the market in that range, over at the marina at the foot of A1A in Dania. He's haulin' his anchor and retiring to the Everglades. If he hasn't already sold his boat, he'll be ready to dicker," 'Soapie' offered.

"I'll take a run over there tomorrow and look it over," Pat answered, "Thanks.".

"Just ask around when you get there. Everybody over there knows Cap Ramos, so you won't have any problem hookin' up with him."

"What about the boats at this marina. I notice 'For Sale' signs posted by three or four?" Pat inquired, trying to make his inquiry as non-committal as possible.

"To be truthful," Soapie chuckled, "I wouldn't touch a couple of them with a ten-foot pole. The 'broker?' handling them has some pretty 'shady' runnin' mates. I'm not sure the papers on them would pass the 'smell test'."

"Oh," Patrick pretended only mild curiosity. "Which boats are those?"

"One's the 'Black Swan', t'other one is the 'Sea Bird'. Don't know where they came from. They just suddenly appeared one morning, tied up and the crew walked off and haven't been seen around since. only the one call's himself a 'Yacht Broker'. MIGHTY PECULIAR!"

The next morning Pat made a visit to the Port Director's office and was allowed to peruse the records of the boat 'Mr. Bucks' was interested in buying.

As he was leaving the PD's office, he noted a pasty-faced character :lounging across the street. His lack of tan told Pat:

"This guy sure isn't from around here," he mused, *"He's definitely new to the Florida Sun. Best keep an eye on him."*

Soapie's' comments about the 'shady' friends and 'Mr. Buck's' warnings gave Pat cause to increase his vigilance. Following a 'street-cop's' breakfast (2 cups of coffee and a couple Krispy Kremes™), Pat took off for the marina 'Soapie' had suggested. He immediately detected a black sedan staying behind him matching him turn-for-turn, but lagging back 4 or 5 car-lengths'.

"Oh, oh," he speculated, *"I think I've picked up a 'tail'!*

His proceeded to take evasive twists and turns in the Florida traffic to throw off the 'tail' he had picked up when returning to his motel. An extra circle of the block before parking in the motel lot assured him that he had ditched any following cars. He parked the 'Spy Mobile' in the back of the motel out of sight of the street.

Patrick spent the morning at the BBB and checking out the local Police Department, where, after identifying himself, was given access to information the average citizen would not be privy to. By early afternoon Pat had amassed a pretty full dossier on the group behind the boat sale.

As agreed, to maintain secrecy, he called Sandy from a public phone, and informed her that he had pretty much wrapped this case. Sandy then called Ian to set up a meet with 'Mr. Bucks'.

Patrick's condo again was decided to be the best meeting place.

As the day was coming to an end, Pat checked out of his motel and cranked up the 'Spy Mobile' and, as he pulled out of the lot, he noted a black Lexus pull away from the opposite side of the street and fall in behind him, keeping four or five cars back.

"This guy is good.," Pat observed, *"I don't know how he found where I was staying, but, here he is, riding my tail! He obviously doesn't care that I know he's there. Well, let's see just how good he really is."*

From the center lane, Pat cut right just inches ahead of the pickup in the right lane evincing an extended play on the pickup's horn. Pat gave the usual 'sorry' wave of the hand and proceeded to make a right turn, leaving the Lexus hemmed-in in the left lane with no way to follow.

The 'Spy-Mobile' shivered and righted itself and sped down the side street. At the first intersection Pat made a left turn, then another left which brought back to the boulevard where Pat fell in six cars behind the Lexus.

"Now' lets see if you lead us back to your rabbit-hole!"

Pat followed the Lexus back towards Ft. Lauderdale. It was no surprise to discover that the culprit led him directly back to the marina. Pat pulled up and parked a block away and observed the driver quickly stroll down the dock to the motor-sailor.

"*I knew you'd been sent by that fake broker,*" Pat hissed, "*I'm convinced, now, that 'Mr. Bucks' was right to be wary of this 'deal'. It smells worse than last week's fish catch!*"

An additional half-hour of quiet surveillance produced no further movement from the men at the marina, so Pat cranked up the 'Spy Mobile' and headed back to his office to type his report. and tally up his time voucher. He stopped to pick up a pizza at Papa Antonio's restaurant for a late afternoon snack.

A shock awaited him when he placed the pizza in the 'Spy Mobile'! an envelope was pinned under the wiper blade. At first glance Pat thought is was a parking ticket, but, before starting up his vehicle, he ripped open the envelope and read the note inside

"You're f . . king with the wrong man, mister! If you queer this deal you'll live only long enough to regret it! BUTT OUT!".

Something wasn't adding up, here!

"*How the devil did he find me so quick?*" Pat mused.

Pat's experience with Chicago traffic was equal to Miami's serpentine boulevards and Interstates so he took a zig-zag route leading into the rear entrance of his condo's parking garage. He sat in the 'Spy Mobile' for an extra ten minutes to check if the Lexus appeared. Apparently his maneuverings had thrown the other vehicle off-track so he rode the elevator up to his apartment with a feeling if satisfaction.

"Screw you, you piss ant. You don't out-fox this Irishman!" as he turned his key in the lock.

He had a couple of hours till time for his meeting with Ian and 'Mr. Bucks' so he soaked some of the stiffness out of his body in his fancy walk-in tub. He pulled on a pair of 'Bermudas' and an aloha shirt, grabbed the pizza, a bottle of chilled Chianti, and retired to his balcony until Ian was due.

"Another day in the confusing life of a PI," he thought, munching on a a huge slice and taking a refreshing sip of his wine.

Ian and 'Mr. Bucks' arrived with the flow of afternoon traffic.

"We've got ourselves a problem, here, gentlemen!" Patrick opened the conversation, "Your phony 'yacht broker' and his pals play tough poker," He informed them, and then proceeded to tell of his little game of 'cat and mouse' he'd been engaged in with the black Lexus, these last couple days.

"It baffled me for a while, how he was able to find me at my motel and then, today, at Papa Antonios', until I realized I'm not the only one with technology in my 'bag-of-tricks!' Just before you got here I went down to the garage and went over the 'Spy Mobile' with a fine-tooth comb. It didn't take much searching to find this little jewel in the right-rear wheel well!"

And he held up a small black box rhe size of a cigarette pack.

"That son-of-a-bitch in the Lexus had 'bugged' my van! These mugs are serious 'goombas!" Pat growled, "I figured out why he lost me just after my stop at Papa Antonio's.

"I still didn't know why I didn't see any more of that Lexus after the 'note' incident. until I got back to my condo. and disassembled the GPS gizmo. I found the button-battery had corroded and stopped putting out juice.

"It was my good fortune that it crapped-out before he'd found my condo. We've a state-of-the-art security system here, but why take chances."

"Pat, me boy," Ian spoke up, "In light of that little note they left, I think we'd best have a little talk with my friends in the Ft. Lauderdale cop shop. I know, 'Mr. Bucks', you wanted this kept quiet, but a threat like that shouldn't be ignored!"

"I'm afraid you're right, Ian. This could get bloody and I don't want any-one gettin' hurt or killed on my account! We'll contact them in the morning and lay it out on the table.

"Detective, you've done an outstanding job. You saved me a couple thousand K. I'm just sorry it went sour and you got caught up in the stew," 'Mr. Bucks' apologized.

"Don't sweat it, Sir, That's just one of the negative sides to being a private investigator. It's why I get the big bucks to afford good insurance!" Pat chuckled.

As an extra precaution, the three took Ian's Honda Accord™ to Ft. Lauderdale for their briefing session with the police.

"Gentlemen," the head of the Fraud Division said, "with all the evidence you have here. We'll be able to bring charges. However, since this also appears to involve the marina in Newport Rhode Island where the craft was obviously stolen, this constitutes inter-state theft so we'll need to bring in the 'Feds'.

"Because of the written threat, I'm not sure gentlemen, if we can keep your identities secret. You WILL have to testify but I'll do a little 'arm-twisting' on the prosecutor and see if we can't work something out on that issue.".

The problem shifted when the Federal Marshalls, warrants in hand, arrived at the marina to find TWO EMPTY SPACES where the mystery yachts had been tied up.

'Soapy' informed the Marshals:

"Yeah, I saw activity on those boats yesterday about sundown. Then, about 11 pm both boats cast off their lines and sailed south on the Waterway They headed for open ocean, with only the required runnin' lights tracing their progress. Didn't think too much about it until you guys showed up here this morning!"

"This does complicate the situation somewhat," Marshall Olsen, rhe lead officer, commented.

"Now we have to start an international search for those scoundrels. They've had enough of a start to be anywhere up or down the coast or even headed for the Islands."

The Marshall's office called Pat and asked him and 'Mr. Bucks' to come in and sign depositions...

"This ought to wrap up the need for you men to be any further involved," Marshall Olsen informed them.

SIX

Sandy had been busy while Pat was involved with Mr. Buck's case.

"I cleaned up a couple 'cheatin' spouse' jobs and an alimony 'skip-trace' investigation," she reported to Pat on his return, "So I haven't been sittin' on my keester ALL the time you were gone."

"You being a licensed Investigator sure has paid off, Gal," Patrick laughed.

"I've decided to take you off salary, Sandy, and I'm cutting' you in for a 33 % of the Agency net.,. Lord knows you've been earning it.!"

"I appreciate that, Boss, But it isn't necessary."

"No discussion. It's a done deal!".

No cases were pending at the moment so Pat declared a three day holiday and locked up the office.

Sandy went off to visit relatives in Cost Rica and Patrick enjoyed relaxing on his balcony with a view. He re-stocked his wine and snack larder and informed Ian his condo was now an 'Open House'.!

"This bit of Heaven is the best medicine for these aching bones," he. informed Ian, "I've been out here since sun up and already feel lke a new man. So, get your butt over here and let's sip, snack and study the beach bunnies. This is too good to waste!"

Ian arrived so quickly, Pat accused him of camping at his front door step.

"What kept you, Cap?" he said, handing him a 'Bud' and leading him onto the balcony.

Ian plopped himself in a lounge-chair, and opened the conversation

"I thought you might like to know, Buddy, your former client found a boat and is enjoying the 'bounding-maine'. After the Feds got through with him he contacted that Captain Ramos 'Soapy' steered you to during your investigation. He was able to swing a deal on a yacht that suits his needs perfectly.

"It's a bit smaller than the 'Sea Bird' if that was it's legal name, but the price was good and Mr. Bucks is content. He sent me this check to give to you. This is <u>in addition</u> to your fee. He's <u>very</u> appreciative of the results of your investigation as you can see from the number of 0000s on the check!"

"Whew! Appreciative isn't the word for it!" Pat gasped. This is more money than a year of my Cop's retirement income!".

"The guy's got too much money and, if he likes to throw it around, you might as well be on the catchin' end," Ian laughed.

With Pat's success solving the 'yacht-scam' case, he now turned his attention to some of the more mundane cases that had been laid at his door.

The case that Pat chose to turn his investigative efforts to first, was a child custody disagreement presented by Lawyer Endicott,

"Detective, my client is involved in trying to establish enough evidence against her estranged husband to get the judge to rule in her favor. She contends that her 'ex' has been inattentive to the child since it's birth and has shown no responsibility in the boy's up-bringing. He's three months in appears in his child-ordered support payments and has only seen the two -year old child once in the year-and-a-half since their divorce.

"We need to establish evidence of his employment and the salary he's made in the two years since the effective date of their divorce. All this will surely cause a new judgment against the errant ex-husband," Lawyer Endicott told Pat,

"We're petitioning the Court to vacate all prior judgments and rule for my client for sole-custodianship of the infant."

"Sir," Pat told the lawyer, "I'll gather what information I can from the records and interviews with friends and neighbors, and if what you've told me can be verified, we should be able to finalize this case in a few days."

"Patrick, I'll need sworn depositions from every one you interview to re-enforce any information they give you," Endicott reminded Pat.

"I'll make sure every thing I uncover will be backed-up by solid documentation," Pat assured the Lawyer.

"Oh, I know it will! That's why I bring my cases to you I know how you work and trust you to present me with a thoroughly prepared rock-solid case."

The following morning, Patrick began his perusing of the court records and making notes. Five hours of thumbing through the complex ledgers at the Courthouse, and he moved on to finding relatives of the wife. He recorded their interviews into his pocket digital recorder for Sandy to later transpose to computer. She would handle typing up the depositions for signatures.

Two days into the custody case and Sandy called Lawyer Endicott to pick up the amassed paperwork.

"Detective Ireland, said to tell you, 'in his opinion it should be a 'slam-dunk'," Sandy commented. "He wrapped up the investigation last night and I've just put the last deposition in the file. It's ready for the Judge when you get the signatures."

"Thanks, Sandy, I'll send a messenger right over to pick up the file. As usual, you people are quick and efficient. Have a good day,"

Wrapping up the final investigative report took him into the wee hours so Patrick slept-in until mid-morning, took a 45 minute soak in his oft-used tub, shaved off a three-day growth of chin-stubble, pulled on his Dockers™ and golf shirt (though he never played golf) and headed for the office.

He was hardly inside the door before Sandy handed him a steaming cup of coffee (laced with a dram of Irish Whiskey).

"Boss, I finished typing up the report you left on my desk, and called Lawyer Endicott. He was pleased we'd closed that one and promised he'd probably have more for us later."

"I have no doubt he will in view of the divorce rate in Southern Florida!"

Sunday afternoon Ian's phone aroused him from his post Sunday dinner nap. It was an urgent call from Pat.

"Cap, I got a problem and I don't know how to deal with it. As you know, I like to spend an hour or so every evening doing laps in our wonderful roof-top pool. It's a great body relaxer and I sleep better after a dip."

"Yeah, Pal, so what's your 'problem'?"

"'Well, the last few evenings at the pool, I've been 'hit-on' by a widow-lady who owns a condo on the 14th floor. I'm flattered but I'm still not over the loss of my wife Flo, and I'm having trouble convincing this rich 'Cougar' that all I want is a platonic friendship.

"She's loaded with millions left her in her late-husband's will, along with ownership of a chain of three night clubs in South Beach. I mean she's <u>Lo.- o- o- o a ded</u>!! She's attractive, has a well preserved figure and would be a great 'catch' <u>IF I was in the mood.</u>

"But I'm NOT! My question is how do I convince her I'm not matrimony-eligible?"

"Buddy, Boy, I've never been in such a dilemma and I'm not the one to advise you. I suggest you ask Sandy for her female guidance."

"I hadn't thought of going to her about this that sounds like an excellent move. Thanks!"

Sandy's first reaction on hearing Pat's problem was to breakout in a nasty laugh.

"Boss, I'm sorry, but I've wondered all along just how long it was going to take for one of these Miami widows to set the net for you.

"Laugh if you will, Gal, but I'm serious. It's very disconcerting to have these predatory husband-seekers bugging me whenever I show up at the pool.

I feel like a side of raw beef hanging on display in the butcher's cooler!"

"Boss, you could tell them you're GAY! That always seems to cool off a man-seeking woman's efforts. I'm kiddin', of course.

"Seriously, I'd suggest you just flat-out say you're not in the market for marriage, but you hope you can still be friends. If that doesn't work, You'll have to avoid her If you can!"

"That's the best you can recommend?"

"Sorry, Boss, but short of drowning her in the pool, YES!"

Spring had come to Miami which meant only a silght change in the climate and <u>no</u> altering of Patrick's routine.

PI inc.'s case-load was light with a smattering of background checks, one or two infidelity surveillance stake-outs and a new issue to work on 'on-line dating' check-ups.

Sandy was a real 'whiz' on the computer so Pat let her handle all the internet 'crap' (as Pat called it).

Pat took on all the surveillance and 'gum-shoe' street pounding cases. He kept the highways and back-roads humming with his 'Spy Mobile'.

Lawyer Endicott and a few other regulars kept the phone-lines buzzing with their civil suites, infidelity investigations, process-serving jobs, etc. All pretty routine.! until a lawyer from Key West called!

"I got your name from Joe Endicott. He gave you high praise for the work you've done for him.

"I'm in need of a good detective to locate an alimony 'skipper' who was last known in your part of the state. He owes about $5K in alimony and child support. If you can take the case, I'll fax the file and his photo to you today. This guy is known to 'carry' so you might have some trouble if he learns you're on to him."

"You know my fees so, if you're still interested, you've got a deal," Patrick told the Key-Wester.

"The info will be on it's way within the hour. I'll include my email address so you can keep me posted. Thanks."

"Sandy, we've got a case for a Key West lawyer so set up a folder. He's faxing us his file. Let me know when it comes in, I want to get on this one while it's 'hot'!"

Patrick lost no time laying groundwork for his search for the defaulter. First stop was an on-line 'people' search of Dade County which was unsuccessful. Then he searched records of Miami/Dade utility companies for new customers still no hits. Next Pat fell back on one of Andy's innovative software programs which lists area motel and hotel residents for the past 30 days. Here he was more successful. A lower class motel in 'Little Havana' listed a resident who fit the description of his target.

All that Pat had to do now was to 'stake-out' the motel and watch until the guy showed. He needed a photo that he could put through his computer 'Facial Recognition' program in order to establish an ID.

Before setting up his surveillance, Pat returned to his office to pick up the fax package from Key West. It contained a photo of the subject along with copies of the, divorce, the Court order for alimony, etc.

"Sandy," he said, "break out the large coffee thermos™ and a sack of snacks. I'm going to be 'campin' out' until I can get this bum's mug in my viewfinder!"

Locating a spot across the street from the motel which gave him a clear view of the room and the office and still offered good concealment, Pat parked his Spy Mobile and settled-in for the wait.

Thirty-six hours and still no sign of hjs 'mark'.

Patrick was patient and spent his time studying the files faxed to him from the Key West attorney.

"This S.O.B. could be paying the alimony without any trouble. "Key West' checked his financials and he's got thousands stashed away. It'll be a pleasure to make him pay up!" Pat murmured to himself, *"He's just one of those 'pinch-pennies'* **A-holes** *who, the more he's got, the more he has to have!"*

On his third day of surveillance, Pat sighted an individual exiting room 15. He matched the description of the suspect so Pat began firing frame-after--frame of photos. With his 400 mm lens he was able to get close-up head shots of several angles of his face and profile. He kept squeezing the shutter until he was sure he had more than enough angles for his 'Facial Recognition' program to make a good comparison. Turning to his Spy Mobile computer, Patrick ran the images through the program and, in fifteen minutes got a 'positive' hit. He had his man!

By this time the man had gotten into his vehicle and driven off too late for Pat to pick up his trail.

"That's OK," Pat reassured himself, *"he'll he back. He took no luggage with him. While he's gone I can take the opportunity to check out his room."*

A 'ten-spot' slipped to the room clerk, got him access and a promise to sound a warning if the roomer returned.

A quick, but thorough, search turned up an envelope containing $20,000 in cash, a bank draft for another 200 K and a passport with a fictitious name. He was apparently getting ready to make a dash for some off-shore country with no extradition agreement with the US!

The desk clerk rang the phone which was a warning for Pat to get his butt out of the room too late! He was sighted leaving the motel room. The guy shouted at Pat:

"You there, stop where you are!"

Pat's thoughts went back to the Key West lawyer's remark **"He's been known to pack"** and it gave incentive for his feet to start tearing up the turf.

As anticipated, shots rang out in the parking lot, and the flying bullets began chipping up the pavement all around Pat's feet. It was Pat's 'Lucky Day', though. The shooter couldn't have hit the broad side of a barn and the Spy Mobile was turning the corner a block away when the final shot pinged off the right-rear fender!

Pat didn't hesitate a single second before calling **911** with a '**SHOTS FIRED**' report. He gave the dispatcher the location and a quick run-down on the sequence of events. He gave her his name, his reason for being at the motel and his P I badge number.

He laid low for 15 to 20 minutes and then slowing returned to the scene, taking a circuitous back-street approach just in case the shooter was still around. By the time the police got there, though, he had cleaned out his room and was roaring away in his Mercedes™.

The all-points bulletin was effective and produced results. The car was intercepted not ten blocks away from the motel. And the shooter was taken into custody after a fifteen minute gun-battle with the police. He sustained minor wounds and was carted off to the Dade County hospital ward.!

Sandy was fit to be tied when she heard of Patrick's run-in at the motel.

"Boss, Why didn't you shoot back at him?" she asked excitedly, "You had your weapon on you, didn't you?"

"Yeah, but that's not the way I operate 'Old Bring-em-Back-Alive Ireland' is my motto!"

"Your 'Bring-em-Back-Alive' motto almost got you KILLED in Chicago, though, you bone-headed Irishman!"

"Well, let's just hope the rest of our cases are tamer and we wont have to worry about 'who shoots first'!"

Pat had Sandy type up a report of their investigation and fax it off to Key West An immediate reply came back:

"Well done, Detective, Fax me your bill, and be generous you earned it! I certainly wasn't expecting to get you into a shootout. Just damn glad there were no casualties on our side!".

Three days on 'stake-out' left Pat with a strong need and desire for a long soak in his magic tub. That's where

Ian caught up with him when he came banging on the door of Pat's condo.

A dripping detective with a wine bottle in his hand greeted him.

"Don't knock the door down, Cap, I ain't in any shape to be rushed!"

"From what I could get out of Sandy, you're lucky to be an any 'shape!

"That poor girl is all broken up over your close encounter with that pistol-packin' crook."

"It was kinda' close, huh? Thank God and that bum's poor aim I'm still around to enjoy my end-of-the-day soak, which, by the way you cut short. with that violent attack on my door"

"Don't get your dander up at me, Buddy Boy, We both care about you and kinda' like havin' you around to sit and sip with on that balcony which by the way is where I'm headed while you get some clothes on!"

"While I'm getting decent you can set out some of that sharp cheddar and wheat crisps. I lost a lot of chow time on this stake-out, and am in need of some nourishment and libation."

A couple of morning walks on the beach, followed by long soaks in his 'miracle tub', and several hours of balcony lounging and bikini watching and Patrick was ready to 'hit the bricks' on his next case.

"Sandy, what have we got on the front burner," Patrick inquired after having his brandy-laced morning coffee, "Any 'juicy' divorce cases that I can sink my teeth into, for a start?"

"That's just about all we do have right now, Boss," Sandy laughed, "It would appear that Miami is full of philandering and infidelities."

"OK. I'll take the oldest one first. I just hope there aren't any gun-happy men or women involved! I've had all the lead-dodging close-calls to last me a hundred years!"

Sandy dug out the case folder and Par sat down to study the information therein.

The case-file only revealed the names of the litigating couple, the lawyer and a very brief synopsis of the complaint.

The husband was suing on the grounds of infidelity. Now it was up to Patrick to gather the facts to prove the charges.

He began by scouting out the wife's movements whenever she was away from home. Parking the Spy Mobile a half-block from the couple's residence and across the street, Pat settled into surveillance-mode.

On the first morning Pat observed the husband leaving for work but there was no further sign of life the remainder of the day. The husband arrived home at 6:30 pm and all was quiet the rest of the night.

"This could turn into a test of my patients," he groused to himself, *"good thing I brought the Big Thermos of coffee."*

The second day started off a carbon-copy of the previous day, so Patrick settled back for another long wait however, at noon, he saw the wife get into her car, slowly back out and carefully head down the street towards the Bayside Marketplace. Maintaining a discrete distance, Pat followed until she pulled into the lot adjoining.

Pat made a 'U' turn at the next intersection and parked on the opposite side of the street. He continued his trailing on foot as she meandered through the Market. She was making a great effort to appear to be shopping until she sat down at a table at one of the sidewalk cafes. She was soon joined by a man who appeared to be somewhat younger. He was dressed in the 'hip Miami' style 'Chinos', 'tank-top' and huaraches.

Pat sauntered past the table and surreptitiously snapped several photos from various angles, careful to avoid detection. Taking a seat on the far side of the café, he watched and waited, recording any moves showing intimacy. So far none of the pictures he'd taken were strong enough evidence to prove infidelity. Their actions, though, indicated, if Pat observed long enough, he'd 'get the goods' he needed.

After an hour of sitting and sipping Cuban coffee, the couple rose and headed out of the Market but *"Damn the luck'* they were leaving by the North entrance! The Spy Mobile was on the South side!

Patrick had no time to get his Spy Mobile. He'd lose them!

Exiting the market, Pat followed his targets east to a parking lot where they climbed into a Ford™ Taurus sedan. Fortunately for him they took a few minutes for some passionate kissing which Pat caught on camera, before he hastily hailed a passing taxi.

"Compadre," he addressed the cabbie, "You keep that blue Ford Taurus in sight. Hold back a few car-lengths and DON'T let them see you! If you don't lose them there's an extra fifty bucks in it for you!"

"Si! Señor!"

Their little trip didn't take them far. The Ford pulled into a space in back of a motel just a couple blocks from the Market.

Pat's driver parked a half a block beyond.

"Wait here until I return," Pat instructed him, "I don't know how long but keep your meter runnin', I'll be good for it!"

"Si, I'll wait right here, Señor."

On foot, Pat, crossed the street and proceeded to approach the motel from the west. He took a seat on a bus-stop bench where he had a line-of-sight view of the couple as they entered a door half-way down the row of rooms. As soon as he exited the taxi, Patrick began snapping pictures of their stroll to the room.

He remained on the bench pretending to read a 'Racing Form'.

The bench was uncomfortable and Pat's still-tender thigh wound was beginning to throb.

"Man, I sure hope you make this a 'Wham Bam, Thank Ya Mam' session,!" Pat murmured to himself.

His wish came true, because after about forty-five minutes the man stepped out, looked around, and motioned for the errant spouse to come out. They quickly got into the Ford and drove back to where she had parked her vehicle.

Pat and his Cuban driver went back to his vehicle and, after settling his taxi bill, accompanying it with a generous tip, Pat waited for the woman to retrieve her car and head back home with the Spy Mobile hot on her tail.

The first thing he did when he got back to his office was download the photos from his camera to his computer and set it to printing copies to go in the file.

While the printer spit out the evidence photos, thanks to the marvel of digital technology, now he could relax and pour a fresh cup of Sandy's rejuvenating coffee.

Sandy finished typing up the report, prepared a copy to send, via messenger, to the client and placed the Master Copy in the 'case completed' folder.

"Another bird has had her wings clipped," Sandy jokingly remarked, as she deftly closed the file drawer.

"The more we uncover, the more pop 'out of the bushes'!" Pat added,

"Tomorrow we start the circus all over again."

"You're right there, Boss. Right now we have three infidelity cases sitting on my desk waiting for one of us to start diggin'."

"Time out for some R & R, first, Miss 'Eager Beaver'. See you Monday. Have a restful weekend."

SEVEN

His daily walk along the beach followed by his usual soak in his magic tub, toned-up his injured leg muscles and Patrick felt fit and rejuvenated.

He arrived at the office on Monday morning rarin' to go.

"Hey, Boss, you look like the week-end charged up your batteries," was Sandy's cheerful greeting, "Bikini watching must have been especially good."

"Yeah, this balmy Miami weather and the gentle surf brought them out like 'flies to honey'. Between that and a half bottle of fine wine, lounging on my balcony and several pleasant naps, I'm ready to hit the ground smokin',

"I've laid out the file on the case which I think takes priority," Sandy told Pat, "it's another case of husband-suspecting the wife of cheating which seems to be the highest percentage of our client load."

"Yeah! I've noticed that, too," Patrick agreed, "I think it's partly because Attorney Endicott has been braggn' us up to his cronies who handle mostly contested divorces. I know he was highly pleased with results of the work he sent our way.

"It's been bringing in the 'green' so I ain't going to turn 'em down. I always said *'If you're GOOD at something CAPITALIZE on it!"*

The case proved to be pretty routine as Patrick began studying the information in the file. The client was requesting a full investigation of hie spouse's actions and personal acquaintances.

Pat began his surveillance by taking up his position on a side street in view of the target's home. Everything appeared to be quite normal A little grocery shopping, a brief visit to the hairdresser's for repairs, stopping at the mini-mart for gas, and back home.

"Nothing, so far," Patrick mused.

Two days of *'Nothing'!*

Patrick was settling in to begin his third day of 'bird-dogging' when his cell phone grabbed his attention. It was the client with news of a change in his wife's schedule:

"She's decided to spend a couple weeks with a friend down in Miami Shores at a 'Spa-Resort' being massaged, working out the 'kinks', and getting pampered. Think that'll be any trouble? I understand they cater mainly to women, so you'll be limited in access."

"No problem. I have a female partner I can send in if we need to observe the activities inside," he was assured by Pat, "Don't worry, If she <u>blinks</u>, we'll have pictures of it!"

"Of that, I'm sure, Attorney Endicott say's you're thorough!"

Patrick and Sandy loaded up the Spy Mobile for an extended stay and were in position when the two women loaded their luggage into their car and pulled out onto the street.

"Sandy, as soon as we scout the Spa and get a 'feel' for the area, I want you to find a nearby motel and book us a couple rooms. we'll work in shifts as much as possible," Pat instructed her, "No need to wear ourselves out. I'll take the first watch."

Two days watching and waiting uncovered nothing of consequence.

"I guess it's time we shift gears and go into PLAN 'B'," Patrick suggested, "We're getting nowhere just sitting out here. We need to find out what's happening inside!"

Plan 'B' called for Sandy to apply for temporary membership, which would allow her access to the facilities. Now she could move about the various 'treatment' rooms under the guise of becoming familiar with what the Spa had to offer. It also gave her a chance to observe the actions of the subject of their investigation.

Each 'Member' was assigned a room with cot and toilet facilities where they would live between treatments. In her quiet surveying of the Spa, Sandy found an interesting item. the target and her companion had booked **adjoining rooms!** This would have been insignificant except, Sandy noted, they seemed to spend their between-treatment time together in one or the other of the rooms never one-on-one!

"Boss," she conferred with Pat, "something's' not right with the picture I get! These two seem to be unusually 'cozy'. You thinking what I'm thinking?"

"I think we have an unexpected twist to this relationship, That's what I'm a-thinking'. Sandy, very discretely ask around among the other members and try to ascertain if our suspicions are right. You know how women like to dish-the-dirt. It shouldn't be too difficult to verify or deny. Just don't 'blow your cover'.

"If we're correct in our suspicions we'll have to report to our client and see how much further he wants us to dig, considering the shift in the wind!"

"Gimme' twenty-four hours, Boss, and I'll milk the facts out of the other members. I've gotten some pretty juicy gossip from these women. They do like to talk!"

True to her word, Sandy was able to record some **incriminating** conversations, as well as sneaking a couple of **VERY intimate photos** through a gap in their cabaña door, showing the two in revealingly indiscretions.

That evening Patrick compiled all their collected evidence and photos for delivery to their unsuspecting client.

"I know this is going to knock him off his rocker. What man wants to find out he's married to a *LESBIAN?*"

Patrick called the client and set up a ten A.M. meeting in his office. He didn't have the 'Heart' to even hint to the client, the secret he and Sandy had run into, A shocker like they uncovered is best reported in person not over the phone!

Their client sat In shocked silence when Patrick laid out the results of **P I, inc.**s' investigation.

"I'm sorry the news is so unexpected," Patrick tried to sooth the shock, "The twist in our investigation threw us for a loop, also!"

"I should have seen this coming." Pat's client remarked, "There were clues popping up every so often during the past five or six months,",

"Another case for the 'completed' file, Sandy, I hope our next case will have a better outcome. I hate it when the good-guy get's the crap kicked out of him (or her)."

"The next job should be a whole lot 'cleaner', Boss," Sandy said, as she fossed another case file on his desk.

"Let's hope so! I'm ready for a 'skip-trace', or an ordinary civil suit. These nasty divorces sure put a kink in one's trust in the honesty of human nature."

Patrick found the 'simple' case he was looking for at the top of the 'pending' file and dove right in getting acquainted with the information it contained.

"This one looks like more of a 'paper-shuffler' and computer data search," He commented to Sandy, "In fact, I'm surprised the attorney couldn't solve his own case and save his client the expense of hiring us!"

"I told him that, when he called, but it appears the client is rollin' in dough and the lawyer decided to help him 'spread the wealth' around a bit!"

"There's no complaint here about collecting a fee for doing the investigating for him," Pat replied, "We'll work the case just as hard as we would under any other conditions."

The case in point was quickly solved with a few phone calls and some data collected off the internet using some of Andy's innovative computer software.

The complainant was being sued over property the county wanted for development. The government wanted to widen one of it's more heavily used cross-town streets and was using the law of 'Eminent Domain' to gain access to several hundred square feet of the complainant's real estate.

P. I. inc. was being asked to probe county records that would back the client's declaration of the assessed value of the property. The client claimed the County was trying to 'low-ball' him in the purchase price offered.

Using the Counties own Tax Rolls, Patrick was able to prove for his client that the County's offer was several thousand dollars below the county's assessed tax valuation.

"As is often the case, the county commissioners were looking to get a chunk of private property at a bargain price," Patrick told his client's attorney"

"Well, Detective, thanks to you, we have the information we need to fight for a fair price!"

"Always glad to see the 'little-guy' get a fair shake," Pat asserted.

"Sandy, dig out the next file and see if we can clear up **TWO** of these simpler cases in one day."

"That should be quicker-said-than-done, Boss.," Sandy replied, "this bundle is thick but the facts are pretty clear and should be easily verified."

Patrick opened the folder and started taking notes. The client was being sued for a simple divorce but the spouse was asking for alimony far outside of the client's financial capabilities. It was up to **P.I. inc** to run a full financial background investigation and bring the demands within reason.

Patrick was able to accomplish this with a few hours of computer work and a couple more of 'paper shuffling'.

"No way your client is able to come up with the kinda' cash the wife is seeking," Patrick told the lawyer, "She's trying to grab funds from a close-held trust fund in their son's name. Your client played it cool,"

EIGHT

Patrick took a break between cases and was catching up on studying the tan-skinned-bikini babes on the beach soaking up the warm Miami sun. He wasn't averse to absorbing some of the afternoon rays himself.

Ian came over and they spent an afternoon being lazy on the balcony, Pat with his chilled wine and Ian nursing a 'Bud'.

"Pat, ol' Buddy, I don't know how you stand this strenuous life-style, you're leading," Ian chided him. "I think I'd wear a hole in that lounge chair if I was forced to park my haunches in it for very long!"

"Yeah, it's a pretty rough life, all right," Pat laughed.

Patrick put on some of his Chicago Jazz CD's and they listened to old favorites from his collection of tunes from the 'Blue Note' and the other South State Street clubs they used to frequent.

"Man, I sure do miss hittin' the live Jazz clubs and diggin' McPartland, Armstrong, Coltrain and the others. CD's are nice but nothing like the real-live stuff," Patrick lamented.

"I hear ya', 'Irish'." Ian agreed.

"South Beach has some pretty 'hip' clubs but I just don't get turned on by the style of music they play give me the good old Chicago sounds, any day!" Patrick commented.

"A-M-E-N! Podner!"

"Boss, we got a 'big money' case that Lawyer Endicott passed off to us. It's gonna' probably require both of us working from both ends.

"Our client has a 'bitch' against a couple big tobacco companies. In his juvie years he developed a heavy smoking habit which lasted for 35 + years.

"About two years ago he stopped smoking but it was too late. Last week he was diagnosed with COPD and first stage throat cancer. He's suing for medical expenses and compensation for future treatment."

"What's the status of the litigation so far," Patrick asked her,

"The tobacco companies are denying their responsibility and have offered a 'goodwill' stipend of $2500. This won't even cover a month's medical bills!"

"You got that right. Sandy, get me copies of the diagnosis and his doctor's, treatment prognosis. We're up against some BIG money interests, and we're going to have to have all our 'ducks-in-a-row', We need to have **solid** evidence if it goes to court. These big industry lawyers have a powerful legal front we're going to have to knock down," Patrick warned.

"I'll over turn every rock in the entire medical community of Miami, Boss. Andy left us with a treasure trove of software dada that will cover any and all previous similar cases and I should be able to pull up plenty cases that show like circumstances."

"While you work the internet I'll be 'hitting the pavement'" Patrick said, "Between the two of us we should be able to get Endicott all the dope he'll need to get a compromised settlement for his client.

"It's a pity anyone should have to suffer like that. No amount of money can compensate for it."

The investigation continued for two weeks and piled up reams of paper reports. In the end, though, the two antagonists reached a just settlement and Patrick and Sandy could close the file.

Clients don't always come to **P.I., inc** by way of a lawyer's referral, The latest investigation presented for Patrick and Sandy, came in the form of a call from a worker seeking assistance in applying for Workman's Comp.

"I'm at a 'road-block' in filing a claim," the client told Sandy, "I've filled out enough forms to pave the Inter-States from here to Orlando. I've collected affidavits from a dozen or more doctors, witnesses and friends and that still isn't enough for those petty bureaucrats. I'm hoping you can light a fire under them."

"I know the frustration in dealing with these government officials," Sandy agreed,

"Detective Ireland and I have been stymied on a few occasions by one of those rare Civil Servants who like to 'feel their oats'.

'We've been quite successful in the past breaking down those walls of resistance, so we'll take a run at it. If we can't clear it up for you, there'll be no charge.

"Come to the office tomorrow," Patrick advised the client. "We'll sit down and you can give us the whole story. We'll work up a contract giving us authority to act in your name, and we'll get right to work solving your problem."

"I've heard good reports about your work," the client commented, "so I'm looking forward to getting my financials straitened out. My medical expenses are draining my bank account."

"Well, we'll try to remedy that."

Patrick and Sandy went to work with the new client, organizing all the paper work he handed them and began laying the groundwork for an all out assault on the 'system-happy' government clerks.

When Patrick encountered the same obstacles his client had run up against he 'took the high road'

"Let me speak to your supervisor!" he insisted. Once again he met resistance

"She's not here today. She's attending a conference downtown. Leave your name and phone number and I'll have her contact you as soon as she finds time."

"OK!" Pat bristled, "Who's in charge until she 'finds time?"

"That would be Mr. Blakley."

"Then, show me to Mr. Blakley's office, because I'm not leaving this building until I get some straight answers!"

"You don't have to get mad.

"Oh, Miss, you haven't seen me **MAD** <u>yet</u>!" Pat hissed, "This case has been knocked around from desk-to-desk for nine months with everyone 'passin' the buck'! So let's quit stallin'!! This applicant is due a fair hearing on this Workman's Comp, and I'm here to see he gets one *if I have to take it all the way to D.C.!*"

The girl jumped up from her desk and scurried off to one of the glass-enclosed cubicals in the rear of the office. She made a hasty return with a short, balding gentleman following close behind.

"What seems to be the problem here, Sir?" he asked Pat, forgoing any greeting. "Can I help you?"

"You're Mr. Blakley, I assume. And YES you can HELP! me! I have here a portfolio of documents that have been submitted over and over during the last nine months, and they keep coming back 'DISAPROVED'!

"I have a Power of Attorney authorizing me to represent the applicant, since he is disabled, and I am petitioning for favorable judgment for Workman's Compensation.

"He has filled out every form you threw at him and all he get's back is MORE FORMS! I informed your clerk here, that I am prepared to take this case all the way to the 'top', if necessary, and this is no idle threat. I only make **promises!**"

"I'm sure this can be resolved, Mr. Ireland, it's more than likely just a case of it not getting into the right hands. I'll have my assistant study the paper work and have this cleared up before the day's over! We have a lounge on the second floor. If you like you can relax there while we get this straightened out."

"Fine, I'll be waiting for your solution. And, by the way that's **'DETECTIVE'** Ireland, for your information!"

As with most waiting rooms (lounges), the reading material and magazines were out of date and dull so Pat used his time going over the files of his present client. With all the facts he had gathered, he was confident the out-come was bound to be favorable.

Results were slow in coming so Pat stepped next door for a quick lunch.

Shortly before closing, Mr. Blakley's assistant ushered Patrick back to his office.

"You've done an impressive job of compiling all this documentation, Detective Ireland. Your client should be pleased to know that our Board Of Review has approved his petition for Workmen's Compensation retroactive to the day of his injury."

"That's great news and I'm certain our client will be happy to hear all the delay has paid off at last, and he can resume a normal life."

As soon as Patrick returned to his office, he picked up the phone and announced to his client the closing of the case.

"Detective Ireland, you and your agency are more than efficient at solving problems. Everything I'd heard about **P I, inc.** was true!"

"Sandy, while we're on a winnin' streak, let's tackle that last investigation."

"Right-on, Boss. This shouldn't be too tough a one to 'crack'. It looks to me to be a simple surveillance and 'tracking' case," Sandy assured him, "I'll dig out the file and we can get started on it first thing in the morning."

"Sounds good to me, Gal," Pat said, "You want to grab a dinner before we call it a day?"

"I could use a Mexican meal to wind up the day, Boss!"

"There's a real authentic Tex-Mex restaurant in the next block," Pat suggested, "how about that?"

"Let me freshen my makeup and I'll be ready for some burritos, tacos and chips and salsa."

"OK, I'll lock up while you do the 'paint-and-powder bit."

NINE

"**T**his case is a 'switcheroo'," Patrick revealed after examining the contents of the folder of their latest investigation.

"Up to now most of our clients have been men searching for evidence against a cheatin' wife this client is the <u>wife </u>with a wandering husband!

"Our client is a missus Raney and has been married to day-laborer, Jeb Raney for seven years. The marriage had been normal and uneventful,. That is, until recently he's taken to spending odd hours 'at work'. His job was usually a normal 8 to 5, but he seems to be spending too much 'after-hour' time at work!"

In her application to hire the services of **P I, inc.** she states her suspicion he is being unfaithful during these extra 'over-time' hours.

"I'll hop in the Spy Mobile and head over to his place of work and see if I can pick up his trail," Pat announced.

The warehouse district, where Raney worked, was a sprawling conglomeration of several 'Butler Huts' and acres of' 'Sea Land' cargo boxes. Before going into the vast complex, Patrick began his search by working up a phony 'Bill of Lading'. With all the different shipping companies represented he was confident that his forged paper work could pass a quick glance.

With his fake papers in hand he proceeded to the yard office. He had to work carefully and make his queries innocent and non-committal to avoid blowing his 'cover'.

Pat picked the most junior-looking clerk and asked her where he might find Mister Raney. The clerk, without asking why he sought him, pulled a clip-board from the many hanging on the wall.

"He's working a heavy-duty fork-lift over in B124 sector." she informed Patrick.

"I'm new here, can you get someone to show me how to get to B124?"

The girl picked up a microphone.

"Bert, come to the office please." she announced.

A short wait and a overall-clad man with a weight-lifter physique stomped into the office.

"Whatcha want, Sweety?" he growled.

"This here gentleman needs to go over to Sector B124. How about showin' him the way?"

"OK. Just follow me in your vehicle, Mr."

The yard worker drove a zig-zag path thru a maze of buildings and cargo-boxes. In the far end of the yard he stopped.

"This here's sector B124 Mr. You think you can find your way out of here?"

"No sweat. Thanks!"

Patrick dismounted from the Spy Mobile and proceeded on foot to scout for the heavy-duty forklift operator, being careful to spot him before he got sight of Patrick or the Spy Mobile.

Patrick was able to locate his quarry and snap several photos without being spotted.

He then returned to his Spy Mobile and left the warehouse yard to park in sight of the gate. There to await his subject leaving at the end of the work day.

When his 'mark' drove out of the yard, Patrick fell into the line of homeward bound traffic. At one point Patrick moved up in the adjoining lane to get a photo of the license plate and then dropped back a few car-lengths to avoid detection.

Raney drove directly home and Pat parked a short distance down the block where he could get an unobstructed view. He settled down and set up his surveillance. That's where he found himself the rest of the evening. No sign of Raney. At midnight he gave up his vigil and returned to his condo.

He set the alarm for 5:30 am and, after a coffee and a quick breakfast, he again took up his position outside Raney's home to begin another day of vigil The routine repeated itself for three more days Still no suspicious moves. Patrick was beginning to think the client had been mistaken.

On the fourth day, Pat cranked up his computer and began a search of the warehouse, looking for anything that might ring a bell. Everything appeared normal. Digging a little deeper into the warehouse records, however, RANG THAT BELL That's where Pat turned up the inconsistency in the inventory figures.

Entries showed periodical disappearance of high-end electronic gear from container box shipments. In the overall picture the losses were miniscule but added up, it amounted to seven figures over the last couple months.

This was enough to cause Patrick to say:

"A-ha! This guy isn't a philanderer he's a common CROOK! But he can't be pulling it off all by himself,!"

Now, his investigation had to shift gears and he started looking for close relationships within the warehouse personnel.

Going back over Raney's personal file and the notes of his four day surveillance, Patrick drew up a list of all of Raney's known associates. The list boiled down to a warehouse night watchman and the senior financial officer in the corporation, a widowed mother of two. The watchman had been employed for seven years, having been hired two years after the CFO. Raney turned out to be the ex-brother-in-law of CFO and was hired on at her recommendation.

"This git's curiouser and curiouser," Patrick mused.

The investigation turned to include gathering and co-relating dates and times of the thefts and how these three were involved. It didn't take Pat long to tie all the facts together and have all the evidence needed to prove the involvement of the three. Patrick called Sandy on his cel-phone.

"Sandy, I've turned up a real 'can-of-worms' in this investigation," Patrick told her, "I'm going to need you to lend a hand. I'm faxing you a copy of the dossier. If what I've uncovered is true, we need to turn the case over to the 'Feds'.

"I'm still going to proceed with my investigation just to determine if our client is involved. I'd hate to see her dragged down with those three. My gut feeling is she's just a poor dupe with a crooked husband!"

Patrick drove the Spy Mobile back to his office and, as he pulled into his parking space, he noted the vehicle he'd been tailing for four days, come to a stop just past his garage.

"This don't look good!" He thought, He picked up his cel and dialed Sandy.

"Gal, I've been 'had'. Get on 911, quick! I'm going to get back in the Spy Mobile and try to throw him off. Keep me on the GPS tracker. I'm heading for the cop house. I don't know how dangerous he is, but according to his dossier he owns a 9mm handgun.

"I don't like the idea of a shoot out, but I'm putting my pistol next to me on the seat. Just to BE PREPARED."

"You BETTER be prepared! Boss! I've grown kinda' used to haviin' you around!"

Patrick took the Spy Mobile on a zigzag evasion course, sometimes loosing sight of his pursuer and then, there he is back on his tail, again.

"Damn, this guy is GOOD! Still several blocks to the cop-shop and I haven't lost him, yet!" Well, here goes nothing'!"

As he approached an intersection he noted there was no traffic so he hit the brakes, turned the wheel SHARPLY and put his van into a spin, As it came around 180° and was headed in the opposite direction, Patrick hit the gas and spun the wheel back and the Spy Mobile was barreling by going the opposite way as his pursuer.

As the two vehicles came abreast shots ricocheted off the back quarter-panel of the van. None of them doing more than minor damage. By the time his adversary got his vehicle turned around Patrick was several blocks away and gaining distance each minute.

Patrick was alighting from his van in front of the police station as the first patrol car pulled in behind him. The pursuer had broken off the chase as soon he saw Pat's van pull up at the police station.

The evidence Pat had amassed was delivered to the local Justice Department and they immediately swore out warrants for the three warehouse employees. The Federal Marshalls wasted no time in rounding them up, and just in the nick-of-time. The three made the mistake of stopping on their escape to gather their 'loot' and the Marshalls cut them off as they were backing out of their driveway.

"When we ran these three through the NCIC list, we turned up four-or five aliases on the two men and an Ohio warrant on the office worker!" the head Marshall informed Pat, "We have two clerks working full time right now, screening cyberspace for any more charges we can lay on this bunch."

Thanks to Patrick's follow up investigation., Missus Raney was quickly cleared of any criminal knowledge of the warehouse thefts.

"Detective, I'm sorry I put your life in danger." she told him, "I never would have imagined him to be the crook that he is. My suspicions only went so far as his philandering."

"Missus Raney don't worry about that. You reacted to his suspicious activities in a normal way. Since the evidence we gathered didn't prove his infidelity, we are waiving our fees. Besides, what we did uncover solved a couple other unrelated crimes. Between the warehouse and the other victims several substantial rewards had been posted We're breaking better than even!"

"Well, it's good to know someone's makin' out in this mess!" she replied, "That S.O.B. of a husband was not only stealin' from his employer but I've learned he about drained our personal finances dry, too! I'm just damn lucky I put a fair bundle away in Index funds in my name. My lawyer tells me he won't be able to touch that, at least!"

"As it turned out, that guy was an 'A-number One' scoundrel, top of the heap, horses' patoot," Pat added.

"And then some," agreed his client.

TEN

Pat was on his second cup of Sandy's special brew when she walked in the office and headed for the coffee pot to pour a steaming cup of brandy-laced 'wake-me-up' for herself.

"You know, Boss," she greeted him as she took her first sip, "Andy's 'Geek-ware' training is beginning to pay off, I was just finishing filing that last case last night, when I got an email asking for a background check on one of those on-line dating services that keep popping up on the TV every half-hour or so."

"Yeah, Doll," Pat took another cup, "That's about all you get on the 'idiot-box' late at night. That and 'miracle cookware' or commercials for gout or depression cure-alls! Ole' PT Barnum knew of what he spoke when he said:

'There's a sucker born every minute'"

"Well, he sure had it right," Sandy agreed, "and they seem to be multiplying like cockroaches. Some may be legit but for every good one on the screen, there's three-or-four 'Gold-Diggers' runnin' scams with new ways to get into your pocket.!

"Back to the email as you're well aware, Miami and the surrounding environs is a 'hot-bed' *(pun intended)* of rich widows 'looking for love in all the wrong places'. That's the plot of the email.

"One of those 'cougars', a Irma Seligman, has latched on to a 'hot-bod' on the internet and want's us to check out him, and the 'dating' web-site," Sandy continued to lay out the scenario for Pat.

"Sandy," Pat spoke up, "You know me and these 'man-eatin' females, I try to stay clear of any entanglements and, believe me it ain't easy! So my part of this is gonna' be strictly investigating the records of the web-site and the male 'gigolos' if that's what they turn out to be. You handle gathering the widow's side of he story!"

"Sounds like a *plan* to me, Boss," Sandy answered.

Sandy seated herself in front of the Andy Jackson-designed computer and started clicking on the keyboard. Under the pretext of a lonely widow looking for companionship, she registered on the 'dating service' that had provided the 'dream boat' for Missus 'S'.

Using phony identity information Sandy was quickly put on the 'sucker list' and given a password 'access code'.

"Boss," Sandy reported when she let the computer cool down,

"Meet the recently divorced Rebecca Allenton of the Cincinnati Allentons. I'm now in line to receive the first five computer matched 'dates'. They're all picked to 'closely fit the profile' I laid out in my application. Now all I have to do is keep checkin' my emails for my soul-mate to start his pitch."

"Sandy, you watch your step and don't forget any one of these on-line lotharios could be a psycho or a sociopath." Pat spoke with concern.

"Don't go all 'Father-ey' on me, Boss, I have a Black-Belt and a lady's 9 mm Berretta both of which I'm well qualified to use if need arises."

Patrick's checks on the 'dating service' and the 'Hot-Bod' were pretty much routine records searches. The BBB had no negative complaints against the male, however the web-site came off wirh only a 'C' rating a mark slightly below 'normal', no real serious marks against them.

However, when Patrick started digging around in the police and financial records of the male escort, he found a few incidents that raised red flags.

"This 'love-boat' has a whole basket full of offenses." Pat told Sandy, "most are misdemeanor crap, but he does have a few charges that bought him some 'time'. a couple 'drunk-and-disorderly' 30 to 60 Days, an assault-and battery case that, since it was against a police officer, got him six months and a year probation!

"None of this information showed up in his web-site profile, so I'd put him in the *'Not a good marriage prospect Box'!!,"* was Pat's assessment.

When they submitted their report to Missus Seligman, she was naturally disappointed but, at the same time relieved that she hadn't been caught up in his scam.

"Detective Ireland, you and Sandy did a great job for me on this case and at the risk of seeming a real 'nut-job' I'd like you to check out one of the other listings the service sent me."

"No problem," Pat assured her, "I think the dating service is 'legjt' so we'll just have to concentrate on getting a clean bill' on this new prospect."

This latest candidate had a 700 + credit rating so Sandy proceeded to scan the internet for any 'red-flags' in his personal or social history.

"Patrick," Sandy remarked, "This guy seems almost too good ro be true. he's got money, well educated handsome comes from good family outstanding military record

"Why hasn't some debutante from Miami's upper-crust snatched him up before now? I even checked out his sexual preferences thinking he might be GAY, but that's not it either.?!"

"Maybe he has halitosis or stinky feet," Patrick laughed

"I'm serious! Boss," Sandy scolded "he's prime meat How has he managed to avoid these Miami 'Man-eaters'?"

"Sandy, Missus 'S' best throw her hook with the best 'bait' into Bay Biscayne, before one of the 'Miami Body Snatchers' reels him in!"

"Pat, you sure got a colorful way of puttin' things!"

"I'm bein' serious, Girl. If she's serious about wanting a man, she'd best step up to the plate! You know the old sayin'

' *A Good Man is Hard to Find!'*

"Don't I know it! Boss! I just might throw **my Sombrero** in this ring, my own self." She joked.

"Hey Chickita! Don't you be thinking' about running off and leaving **P. I, inc**. high and dry, You're what keeps this this machine hummin'!"

"Only spoofin' Boss, I need a man like I need a hole in the head. As I told you when you took over this Agency:

*"I'm single, unattached and **liking it!"***

As a result of **P I, inc.**'s background checks for the online-dating web site, they began to receive more requests for more applicant investigations.

"In the final analysis it saves time and avoids possible law-suits by eliminating the riff-raff," the web manager informed Pat.

"We welcome repeat customers," Pat responded, "especially background checks that just about complete themselves."

"The computer programs invented by Andy make these kind of searches child's play." he informed Sandy,

With the influx of the regular dating-service work, Pat and Sandy settled into a day-to-day routine Sandy punching data into the computer and Pat handling the cases requiring leg-work.

Since the work-load was so routine, Pat was spending his leisure-time parked on his balcony enjoying the Fabulous Florida climate.

It was on one of these laid-back days that he rang up Ian and invited him to join him.

"You remember one of my early clients, the one who only wanred to be known as 'Mr. Bucks' who we saved from being scammed in a crooked boat-brokerage deal?.

Well, he's back in Florida and gave me a call Tuesday. He asked me to come over to the marina where he's moored, he had a souvenir for me.

"While he's been sailing up and down the coast he did some lobstering up around Mystic and had filled up his bait tanks with 50 to 60 nice meal-sized crustaceans and I should drop by and take some off his hands.

"You and your missus need to come over Saturday and we'll have a good ol' 'Lobster Boil'. I got all the fixins' a case of 'Bud' cooling in the 'fridge, plenty of fine wine, and all the stuff for coleslaw. We'll sit back and 'pig-out'!"

"Hot Damn, Li'l, buddy You got my taste buds stirred up! Only thing is, Sally is allergic to shell-fish, but she's all wrapped up in one of her fund raisin' charities Saturday, anyway so that just means you and I'll just have to make pigs of ourselves woe is me!"

"Cap, there's times when a man just has to suffer for the cause!"

After stuffing themselves with succulent lobster and washing it down with cold 'Bud' and chilled wine, Pat and Ian settled back to observe all the bikini-clad beach-bunnies.

"Patrick me boy," Ian spoke up, "one of my golfing buddies hit me up the other day with a problem which I think might be up your alley.

"It seems his 23 year-old daughter has takin' a likin' to a thirty-year-old guy of questionable motives. He want's him thoroughly checked out!

"He's heard some rumors about the guy and he want's to make sure his daughter isn't going down the wrong road."

"No problem, Cap," was Patrick's response, "just give me his name and any details he already has about the man and I'll start a search when I get back in the office Monday morning.

"If he has <u>any</u> kind of a record Andy's software will ferret him out!" Pat promised.".

"Thanks, 'Irish', I knew I could count on you. This concerned father has ple-e-e-nty of dough so I'm not asking any favors in that respect.!"

"Gotcha! 'bill as normal' it'll be."

"Cap, I'm goin' to the kitchen, how about some more lobster? There's a pot full left and what we don't finish-off today I'm gonna' chop up and make some good ol' lobster salad for sandwiches to have for snacks the next few days."

"Yeah, I'll have another claw to munch on. Those claws are a large hand full. I'm also ready for another 'Bud'."

The sun was moving over the western landscape and the 'Bikini Bods' were beginning to gather their blankets and abandon the Florida beach. With the main attraction departing, Pat and Ian finished off their final lobster snacks and they also retired from the balcony to the comfort of the living room.

"I guess I'd best be heading home, 'Partner'," Ian announced., "Sally likes me home when she returns from one of her charity soirees."

"I'm with you where those 'Hen - parties' are concerned," Pat chuckled. "any time you get left home alone, though, Cap, I always have a few 'cool ones' sittin' in the 'fridge and the view is usually pretty interesting most afternoons. You can always hang out over here.!"

"I'll take you up on that, Pal, but I might get some 'static' from Sal if she ever get's wind of how we spend our balcony lounging time!," Ian laughed.

"See ya' Pat."

Monday morning Patrick clued Sandy in on the latest case and they began working the ol' internet for any evidence pro-or-con on their subject.

Sandy was the first to get a 'hit' on the daughter's love interest.

"Pat," she commented, "so far the man looks pretty squeaky-clean but I'm going to dig deeper. Nobody goes for 38 years without even a traffic ticket!"

"Have at it, Girl! I want to know if he ever spat on the sidewalk, cursed in church, or picked his nose at the dinner table! Everyone has some kind of ghosts lurking in their closet. So, good or bad I want it in the report."

"Roger! Boss!"

Three days of diligent search uncovered nothing negative about the man, so Patrick turned over a favorable recommendation to their client.

"All I can say," Pat told Sandy, "if I had a daughter I should hope she'd find such a man,".

ELEVEN

"**S**andy, I'm thinking' it's about time for a bit of a vacation." Patrick announced, "we've had our noses to the grindstone pretty continuously for the last nine or ten months, and, I don't know about you, but I'd like a break from snoopin' into other peoples' lives.

"I'm gonna hop a plane and visit my sons out in Oregon for a couple weeks. Why don't you fly down to Costa Rica and spend some time with your family? Bill the ticket to **PI, inc.** You've earned a bonus. We'll just lock the door and turn off the phone!"

"Boss, you must have been reading my mind," Sandy added, "I was talkin' on the phone just the other night with my cousin, and she asked when I was going to come see her and the rest of the clan."

"So let's DO IT!" Pat declared, "Stay safe and enjoy your visit. I'll see you in a couple weeks!

Pat's twin sons met him at the Portland Air Terminal with much back-slapping and hugs. After gathering his luggage he was ushered to Tony's car and they headed south along the Willamette River to Tony's home in the little town of Cottage Grove.

"Dad," Tony announced, "I hope you like fishin', cause Salmon is in season and we're within shouting distance of the Mackenzie River which has the best run of salmon in the northwest.

"The rest of the family are meeting us at my place. Robert's place is about twenty miles up the river in Oak Ridge so we're going to all congregate at my house. Saves running back and forth and wasting time on the roads."

"These woods and mountains are beautiful. South Florida is flat and our 'mountains' are only about thirty or forty feet above sea-level!

"Boys, the smell of the Douglas Fir trees is intoxicating. I see why you like it here!"

"Well, there's plenty room up here. Leave Miami and move to Oregon."

"It'd be tempting but I have a comfortable condo with a nice Atlantic Ocean view and a growing business. I think I'll pass on the invite."

Tony's house was a large four-bed-room log structure set back from the road in a stand of tall firs, and was presently crawling with the gathered Ireland family members.

A long table and benches were set up under the trees and the table was loaded down with a sumptuous meal.

The Oregon members consisted of two pre-teens on Tony's side and one grade-schooler belonging to Robert.

The animated conversation and the chatter of the three children echoed throughout the trees and continued until long after the meal was finished and the dishes cleared.

In the morning Tony and Robert hitched up the boat to Robert's van, loaded Pat and the two oldest boys aboard and headed for the River. By noon they had hauled in their limit of Mackenzie River salmon and were headed back.

"I never saw so many huge fish fighting to get into the boat, before!" Patrick marveled.

With more fishing and hiking, the vacation days passed quickly and Pat's vacation quickly dwindled to a close.

"You now owe me a visit," Pat declared, "but, other than swimming and walks on the beach, I'm afraid I can't offer the excitement of fishing the Mackenzie and hauling in a gigantic salmon."

"If we go to Florida we gotta' stop off at Disney World!" the three children piped up in near-unison.

"Oh, yeah," Pat answered, "My place is only a short run up the Turnpike. Let me know when you're coming and I can use my connections to get you reservations and tickets."

Patrick was soon back to the old grind, again.

Sandy's return to the office came two days later and she checked in with a cheerful:

"Hi, Boss, Hope your vacation was as great as mine. I sure hated for it to end."

"I had an outstanding time caught a batch of Oregon Salmon and ate my fill of real 'woodsman' vittles," Pat replied, "Now it's time to get back into harness and start tracking and snooping."

The 'tracking and 'snooping' soon began with a phone call from Attorney Endicott.

"Hey, Friend," Pat greeted him, "what can **PI inc.** do for you, today?"

"Oh, I have a 'doozey' for you this time. It might be a bit of 'touch-and-go' cause it calls for investigating a Deputy Sheriff and the County in a law suit. My client is suing for false arrest, illegal detention and tampering with evidence."

"Wow! Sounds like 'Deep-throat' in the south. Why don't we have a face-to-face and you can brief me. How about Juan's Coffee Shop at 10 AM? That's about half way between your office and mine."

"Fine, I'll see you there. Bring that beautiful partner of yours along. She might be of use in carrying on surveillance without arousing suspicion.

The three settled down for a cup of Cuban Coffee and Lawyer Endicott began to lay out the details:

"My client is a student at Georgia Tech and was home on Spring Break when he was pulled over on the Florida Turnpike by a Reserve Deputy Sheriff for an obscured License Plate (Georgia mud splatter over some of the numbers).

"The student was cooperating but the Deputy was 'feeling his oats' and insisted on frisking him and searching his car. From the glove-compartment he withdrew a bottle containing three Oxycodone tablets. Despite the clear label showing the medication's prescription for pain due to a rugby injury, the young Deputy confiscated it and took it in evidence charging the student with 'illegal' possession of a controlled drug.

"Handcuffed and hauled him off to jail where he was held for a hearing before a judge. It being Friday, no judge was available to rule on the case, consequently my client had to spend three days and three nights in jail.

"To compound the 'comedy of errors' the green Deputy neglected to file the arrest-warrant until Wednesday leading to <u>TWO</u> more days and <u>Nights </u>in a cell!

"Man, I'd say your client has a cut and dried case. What is it you want us to investigate?"

"Under most circumstances it **would ** be 'cut and dried' but, the Sheriff's office is ignoring the facts and has written it all off as 'a mistake by a green officer'.

"My client's family is the well to do, prominent Neuton family of Miami and are not letting it be swept under the rug!

"I need you to dig into the records in the possession of the Deputy, the Sheriff's department and the County Prosecutor. That's going to take some sneaky maneuvering to gather the goods without arousing dust in the department," the lawyer warned, "something 'stinks-in-Denmark', so to speak, and I need someone like you to unearth the bodies."

"I follow your drift, Counselor!" Patrick assured he lawyer, "We'll get the ball rollin' right away.

The first stop Patrick made was to interview young Ralph Newton for his version. Nothing they learned from him differed from what his lawyer had recounted to Pat, so the next step was to start some discrete inquiries within the Department. Trying to question personnel within the law-enforcement family produced mostly non-committal answers 'no comments' all around.

"The outcome was a 'monkey see no evil, monkey speak no evil' attitude," Patrick told Sandy.

Other deputies in the arresting officers' Academy Class, not assigned to the same district, revealed the Deputy's apparent dislike for those 'spoiled college namby-pambies', and drew Patrick's concern as to the patrolman's mental attitude. He was reported to have a 'short fuse' and a 'sharp tongue'.

Pat also found out that he was lax in his paperwork and disliked all the pen and pencil work involved in filing his records.

A week into the investigation, Sandy, working the computer search and Pat doing the interviews and the 'leg work', led to Lawyer Endicotts conclusion that he had sufficient evidence to proceed with his suit.

"Another well done for **PI inc.**", Attorney Endicott said when he handed Pat his check.

"Good Luck on you suit. Counselor," Pat replied.

"Sandy, I think this calls for a celebration. This has been a very successful three years and, with your help, **PI inc.** has gained a reputation for coming through where civil law needs a boot!. How about dinner in that Turkish Restaurant near my condo? I tried it out and highly recommend their native dishes."

"I think I'd lke that, Boss. I've always enjoyed some of that Middle-eastern cuisine."

"Turkish it is then," Pat announced.

A couple days rest and another case was logged into **PI inc.'s** pending assignment sheet.

This latest came by way of an email from the dating service client for which Pat had previously done background checks.

"We've been apprised of several scams perpetrated on some of our subscribers," the message read, "this has effectively harmed our dating record and has taken several of our subscribers for thousands of dollars.

"We need to uncover who is doing this and how it's being done.!"

Sandy emailed the web-site manager and arranged a face-to-face at the **PI inc.** office.

The web's manager and customer service director brought all their records to the conference and Pat and Sandy began compiling lists of victim's names and incidents of the fraudulent actions.

"I think we have sufficient info to start our investigation," Patrick announced, "we'll keep you apprised off our progress as we go along.

"Have local police or other law-enforcement agencies taken any action on the case?"

"No," the web manager responded, "they say they're not equipped to handle 'cyber-crime', and since all the action has been carried out by email, civil action is about the only way we can nail these crooks."

"OK," Pat replied, "You need to line up a good civil lawyer then and, when we have completed our investigation, we'll turn over our report to him for action."

"Be sure he's <u>well up on internet law,</u> because this case will be establishing new precedents and breaking new ground!" Sandy advised.

"I'll get on the computer and start digging around for any past similar cases that we can reference."

"Yeah, Sandy, right now we don't know how extensive this operation is, so we need to compile all the evidence we can**. 'Snow 'em under with FACTS!'** " Patrick advised.

Sandy's efforts resulted in revealing five men had been taking money from elderly on-line members to the tune of $700,000 + and were still operating their scams on a daily basis.

"Pat, they're really computer 'savy'," Sandy reported, "they're shifting their cyber-bases after each 'hit', So far I've been about two moves behind them but I think I can pin them down on their next couple of moves!"

"OK, Gal, I'm going to bring in the 'big guns'. Andy left me one of his original software programs that's supposed to head off those 'moves'. I haven't had occasion to load it up before now, so let's see what it does!"

"Boss! It worked! I got names and addresses on two of those thieves and Andy's program is closing in on the other three like Superman carrying **a lightening bolt**. I should have the rest of them located before tomorrow!"

"Good on ya, Sweetheart!" Pat shouted!

True to her estimate, Sandy had nailed the details on the last of the gang and the lawyers for the on-line dating service filed their suits.

Once they had **PI inc.'s** investigative evidence report, the Federal Marshalls moved in and gathered up the group and put them in the lock-up.

"Now that we know how to go after them on the internet, we should be able to work the internet more effectively in future cases," Sandy informed Patrick. "That program that Andy wrote is worth it's weight in GOLD!

TWELVE

Ian and Pat were spending another warm Florida afternoon sipping cool-ones and studying bikinis.

The office of **PI, inc.** was closed for the weekend and the two ex-Chicago cops were marveling at the gap between the Chicago December temperature and Miami's spring-like 72°.

"Think it's goanna snow, Cap?" Pat asked, facetiously.

"Maybe in Chicago, but I doubt we'll ge any here!"

"A day like this we ought to be in the pool or patrolling the beach," Pat commented.

"OR Slopping up a cool 'Bud' and frosty glass of Rhinecastle and enjoying the oil soaked bodies populating the beach!" Ian voiced his opinion.

"You been getting any of that senior 'nookie'?" he queried, "The last time we laid out near your condo pool there seemed to be quite group of attractive 'huntresses' eyeing us."

"I'm still getting the 'come-on' from a few of the silver-haired singles here at the pool, but, up to now I've been able to dodge their nets," Pat informed Ian, "My single status is threatened every time I take a dip!

Only my enjoyment of 'bachelorhood' has sustained my resistance to their temptations!"

"Well, hang in there, Irish, the male psyche can withstand such enticements just so long!"

"Thanks, Pal! A bit more moral support from you would be appreciated!" Patrick noted.

"Boss, we've been handed a case of 'Irish Sweepstakes' to investigate for a Miami widow. She's already been cleaned of $75,000 and got tired of being 'nickle-dimed' at every turn," Sandy said.

"Yeah, I've heard of these scams, but I thought they were out-dated long ago. A decade ago the mail was saturated with these 'come-ins' snd then they disappeared from the scene. The internet just opened a whole new can of worms and I guess now people need to be re-educate!" Pat responded.

"The old system of 'milking the marks' has a new face but the enticements are still the same. 'GET RICH' quick and easy!" Sandy agreed.

"Right, First, you get an email stating :

"Your name has been drawn in a (fictitious) 'IRISH SWEEPSTAKES' but to claim the prize the winner needs to forward X- amount of dollars to cover taxes (or postage)."

"If you take the bait, you get another message with another request for $ $ for some other nefarious expense," Pat added.

"This keeps up until you stop sending money or you start askin' too many questions. suddenly the web site disappears!"

This new client is asking **PI inc** to search out the perpetrators and, if there are any US connections, gather information sufficient to prosecute the crooks under US Fraud codes.

Sandy went to work on the computer, tracing any trail the scammers might have left behind. They were clever in setting up firewalls and hiding servers but Sandy, using another of Andy's programs, hacked into their cyber shuffling and narrowed the path down to three individuals in Philly.

"I'm turning all our evidence over to the Feds for follow-up and charging," Patrick told Sandy, "Our client informed me that she wants to press charges against these swindlers. Hopefully the Federal Prosecutor can put them out of business, dig a hole under the jail and shove these crooks under it."

"It's impossible to recover any of the money these shysters have already collected, but, maybe we can make them pay with some jail time and save the next gullible fish from falling for the bait!" Sandy lamented.

"Back in the '60s, when I was still on the force in Chicago," Pat recalled, "our Fraud Division came up with a 'reverse-sting' and cleaned out a gang pulling this fake sweepstakes racket. They managed to not only put them out of business and put the perpetrators in the 'clink' but they confiscated a big chunk of cash and holdings the gang had accumulated. "Wish I could remember just how the 'sting' worked, maybe we could rope in this Philadelphia gang. But all those guys from our old Fraud Division have long since moved on, though, and it might not work in a cyber environment, anyway."

More and more **PI inc.**'s case-load involve extensive computer searches. Thanks to the former owner of the agency, Andy Jackson's innovative, programs, **PI, inc.**'s computer prowess far exceeded most local law enforcement capabilities it was only equaled by the **FBI** or **CIA** and maybe one or two foreign intelligence agencies.

Sandy had mastered the computer searching and cases turned over to **PI, inc.** got quickly resolved.

Where surveillance is needed to establish the client's cause, Pat used the vast capabilities of his 'Spy Mobile a normal SUV also converted by Andy with cameras (digital and night-vision), lenses from macro-to-extreme telephoto, a state-of-the-art computer and printer and the capability to transmit data and photos to any computer in the world.

All these items are, in one way or another, the result of the genius of **PI, inc.** s' former owner. a 'GEEK' above 'Geeks'.

"Sandy, I don't know where we would be as an investigating agency if not for that Man!" Pat commented to his partner.

"Boss, you sure got that RIGHT!" was Sandy's response.

"Speaking of Andy, one of his former clients emailed us the other day asking for our services.

"He has a law practice in the Miami suburb of Hallendale. One of his clients contacted him to investigate his missing wife and seven-year-old daughter. It's one of those upshots of a messy divorce. The client, Mr. Rick Baldwin, was awarded joint custody of the daughter and now the ex and his child can't be located.

"One of his fears is that the ex-wife, being a foreign national (Ecuadorian), has probably fled to her native country with the girl.

"Sandy, This case is going to have to be best handled by you since you are fluent in Spanish, Contact with the Ecuadorian officials is going to call for co-operation between them and our government.

"This is going to step on the toes of some diplomatic 'big-wigs' and we need to tread lightly!" Patrick instructed Sandy.

"Patrick I'm going to have to dig deep into Ecuadorian civil law. This is unfamiliar territory so 100% of my time will be required to just 'lay the groundwork' for a custody case."

"I know that, Sandy," Pat affirmed, "You take all the time you need and spare no expense this client is loaded and says he'll pay ANYTHING to get his daughter back!"

"Swell, cause I'm sure there's going to be one or two trips to Ecuador to establish a liaison with their government and law enforcement officials down there," Sandy added.

"According to our client, the mother has family connections to some of the shady side of Ecuador's underworld and there's almost certainty they won't give up the child quietly," Pat warned, "I've applied to the State Department and the Ecuador Government for you to carry a concealed weapon, so go out to the range and polish up you shootin' eye. BE PREPARED!"

"I've kept up my weapons qualifications but I'll be sure to put in some extra practice, in the meantime."

Sandy, as promised, spent the next week at the local library 'boning' up on Ecuadorian civil law and several hours at the Miami police range firing her Beretta 9mm.

Now began the investigation process.

The client and Sandy sat down for two days for Sandy to absorb the details of the case. Finally, Sandy felt she had sufficient info to begin seriously searching for a mode of operation in the investigation.

Initially she questioned any and all of the local friends and acquaintances of the missing wife. She followed that up with checks of the child's school and health records, looking for any recent changes. Exhausting these sources only proved that the fugitive wife had indeed returned to Ecuador. All information gleaned from these sources was logged and entered into the computer data-bank.

When she was sure she had all the evidence available in Miami she decided it was time for a trip 'south of the border'.

Checking in with the local police, Sandy was warned about the wife's relatives:

"Señorita," El Comandante of the local barracks of Ecuadorian Policia Nationale warned Sandy. "The Esposito clan are a dangerous familia to cross. Son Muy aburrido gente (tr. *dangerous croud)*! hace cuidado (*be careful)1*"

"Gracias, Comandante."

Sandy was turned over to an Ecuadorian interpreter to 'better communicate' as the officer put it (not knowing Sandy spoke fluent Spanish).

Ortego, the interpreter, escorted Sandy to a safe hotel and got her safely put up for her stay in his country.

He bid her "Buenas Noche" and left her with the instructions that he'd pick her up in the morning.

Sandy spent a fitful night's sleeep fighting the anxiety of the coming day's events.

Ortego was knocking on her door almost before the tropical sun had peeked through the palms outside her room.

A quick breakfast of black coffee, fruit and pastries and Ortego wheeled the vintage Mercedes-Benz onto the road into the suburbs where the Esposito Hacienda was.

"Señorita, I'm taking you on a short tour to let you see where the family lives. Getting inside can be suicide as they have a virtual fortress from which they conduct their various illegal operations.

"I'd also be very careful who you trust in Ecuador as they have the town covered like a spider's web. Even we police have to be careful, as your best friend'll turn you in for favors from the Espositos. TRUST NO ONE!"

"I must say, Señor," Sandy said, "it sounds to me like this mission is looking more like a 'SEAL' operation than a simple child recovery job."

"It won't be 'simple'," Ortego chuckled, "But, if we watch long enough, these kind will stub their toe and we just have to be ready to make the 'grab' when they do."

A visit to the US Embassy set Sandy's plan back. The Embassy legal Council advised her of an unexpected technical glitch.

Sandy immediately emailed Patrick:

"Need you to bring our client to Ecuador ASAP! Ecuadorian law dictates that the <u>complaining parent </u>be present in order to remove the child from the country. Otherwise we're up against KIDNAPPING charges. Officials here are cooperating but the law is the law!"

Patrick immediately contacted the client and they caught the earliest flight to Ecuador. Sandy and her interpreter met them at the airport and the four proceeded to the US Embassy to announce the arrival of the child's father.

"I'm afraid we can't officially intervene so the operation will have to be carried out without any assistance from us," the Embassy's Legal Council advised, "All I say is : *'Good Luck!"*

Now began a waiting game Sandy and Patrick took turns keeping an eye on the Esposito compound. If they left the house to go shopping or to the beach or anywhere outside the grounds, the 'rescuers' were ready to put their plan into action.

So far the presence of the investigators had been kept a secret, but, in a close society like this a 'leak' can spring without notice. Consequently they had to be ready to move without hesitation.

Two days three days nothing!

Then, the family car left the grounds and headed to a favorite family restaurant for an evening meal.

<u>"OK, Sandy, time to move on 'em!"</u> Pat ordered, "I've arranged for the local police to set up a diversion as the family leaves the restaurant that's when we make our 'grab'.

"There'll be a plane warming up as we speak. TIME is of the essence so every move has to go off without a second's hesitation! If there's any shooting try to hold your fire until absolutely necessary. Then, aim to distract rather than kill! We can't afford a murder rap in a foreign country! "Right now the law is on our side, let's keep our skirts clean and we'll be free and clear!"

As the family was leaving the restaurant an Ecuadorian Police car drove up and parked in a space in front of the two Esposito Limos. The officer did not get out of the car just sat there smoking, unconcerned. The girl lagged behind her escorts a couple of feet that's when Sandy swooped in and quickly snatched the girl and Pat moved between the girl and the Esposita adult diners, separating the party from Sandy and the girl.

With the surprise and the shock of the unexpected attack dis-combubilating' the Esposito party, Patrick and Sandy, with the girl under her arm, took advantage of the confusion and piled into their car and Ortego made a screaming takeoff on a circuitous route for the waiting plane.

The action took the Esposito body-guards precious seconds to figure out what had happened and to react. They got off a couple shots at the fast vanishing Mercedes-Benz until Señior Esposito shouted:

"STOP SHOOTING! You idiots! You might hit the girl!

By the time the Esposito cars could maneuver out of the blocked-in space and exit the parking lot, Sandy and the Mercedes-Benz were unloading their precious cargo into the plane and it was speeding down the runway, lifting wheels and heading **north!**

The seven-year-old was still in shock but as soon as she saw her father in the seat beside her, she cried out in joy and showered him with hugs ad kisses.

Another success for **PI, inc.!**

THIRTEEN

Background checks were becoming the major investigation cases for **PI, inc** and Sandy was on the keyboard almost the entire day. The programs that Andy had modified made quick work of most searches, but, the more cases Sandy was able to run, the more seemed to come in.

"Sandy," Patrick told her, "Concierge at my condo has asked for my help in doing security around the building and I'm considering turning the most part of our Agency over to you.

"With the work the online dating service has called on us to handle, I don't see any advantage to doing. any more spousal conflicts, civil suits, or surveillance cases, etc. They don't pay as well as our background searches when you compare time/charges involved.

"My condo management has offered to waive my monthly management assessments in exchange for my infrequent security service, which sounds like a 'sweet' deal. I'll sign over the **PI inc.** operating license to you and I'll just remain in an 'advisory' capacity.

"What do you say, ___*Detective*___ Sandy?"

"Boss, I don't know what <u>to say</u>!" Sandy replied, "Do you really think I can handle the agency all by my 'lonesome'?"

"Hell yes, Gal. You and Andy's computer programs practically run this business right now, without me sticking my finger in the pie!"

"That sounds like a fine arrangement for you, Boss. I know you're getting burned out chasing all these 'nimwits' around Miami. This way you'll have more time to enjoy your pool and balcony.

"Personally, I think you ought to write a book about your Chicago and Miami adventures, and now you'll have the time."

"WHOA up, there, Little Lady, I still don't see me sittin' over a hot keyboard, braggin' about Patrick Irelands' nefarious exploits.!"

"Shoot, Boss, it'd be a 'best seller' for sure!

"If you can't 'write' it record it and have someone else type it up, or dictate it! You have enough 'tall-tales' in you to fill volumes!"

"I'll have to do a whole lotta' brain-stormin' on this before I take on such a tall piece of work!"

"Give it some of that ol' Irish mental effort, Paddy, and you'd be surprised what'll boil to the surface.

His Chicago buddy Ian was taken by surprise when Patrick informed him of his change of plans.

"I had a hunch **PI inc.** was going to wear thin after three or four years (didn't expect you to last <u>Five</u>, though), It's about time you start enjoying the 'fruits of your labor', Irish", was Ian's comment.

The deal offered by the condo manager (or 'Concierge' as he liked to be referred to) appealed to Patrick in it's simplicity.

"All I'll have to do," Pat described it to Ian, "is cruise the corridors on the four-wheeled electric cart they're providing and look for troubles any of the residents might be having, security-wise.

"A piece-of-cake!" Pat wrapped up.

"Pat, Me Boy, I don't know where you came by all your good luck, but I sure wish some would rub-off on me." Ian laughed.

"The 'concierge' also said I might want to also sub-contract with some of the 'Snow-Birds' and pick up a bit of extra change 'apartment-sitting' for them while they travel or spend their summers up North. It would entail checking their apartments occasionally and collecting their mail and forwarding the non-'junk-mail' to them."

"I guess you'll find plenty of 'balcony-time' on your hands, now, huh?" Ian chuckled, "I hope you keep the welcome-matt out so I can keep up on you and your 'strenuous' life-style,"

"Cap! I'll keep the liquor-locker and the snack bar stocked and I expect to see you parked out here or up at the pool just as often as Sally slacks up on the leash. I'll need your company to keep the boredom-bug from my door," was Pat's quick reply.

With a bear-hug, Patrick handed over the keys to **PI inc.**, and turned to his new duties as Condo Security Officer.

"Sandy," he advised her, "If you need occasional detectin' help any time, I'm still your backup guy!"

"Boss., working with you has been the best training any aspiring PI could get at any price!" She praised him, "Your vast experience and Andy's innovative computer programs practically solved the cases without any effort on my part!"

"You'll DO, Gal, You'll DO!"

Patrick spent the next couple weeks getting briefed on the condo building's layout and being introduced to the other tenants.

The idea of having a professional investigator on premises was met with overwhelming approval by all the condo owners.

"Detective Ireland, having you in the building takes a load off the minds of most of us especially we snow-birds. We've been paying outside security agencies far too much for limited patrols and sparse protective services," was the comment by one old time condo owner.

"Many of us relied on our full-time neighbors to 'kinda' keep an eye' on owr property while we were absent! Not always that effective!"

"From now on, I'll want anyone who is planning to be absent more the 48 hours to log out, and back in, with the concierge, so I can make extra checks on those apartments on my rounds," Patrick instructed the tenants.

"VIGILANCE IS PROTECTION
is my watch-word!" he told his condo clients.

Patrick's new duties as Resident Condo Security Officer left him with plenty of leisure time. At various intervals during the day he made a cruise through the hallways touching base with residents along his route.

He enjoyed meeting all the neighbors whose friendliness mirrored his own with only one exception the grouch in apartment 403 North.

The bachelor seemed to have a complaint about everything and everyone in the building.

"I think his face would shatter if he tried to smile," Pat commented to the concierge.

"You're so right, Pat.

"I think he wakes every morning with a burr under his saddle! He's impossible to please."

"Well, I firmly believe a smile and kind word can break down most walls," Patrick replied,"

FOURTEEN

Five weeks into his new job, all was smooth sailing. Patrick was liking it more and more, but things changed suddenly one morning!

Making his early inspection rounds of the roof-top pool he was shocked to note a <u>body floating face-down</u> in the deep-water end of the pool. He rushed over for a closer inspection and became immediately aware the 'floater' was beyond reviving.

As proper police work dictated, he didn't disturb the body but quickly dialed **911** and reported hs find. He made a second urgent call to the front desk, and waited by the pool for the police and coroner to take charge of the scene.

The concierge rushed to the pool as quick as the elevator could ascend the seventeen floors.

"Victor," Pat cautioned the condo official, "We need to secure the crime scene and touch nothing until the police take over. No one comes on this floor!"

"What makes you think it's a 'crime scene' Pat?"

"If you look close you'll note there's some blood in the water near the victim's head, and I don't see any on the pool's coping. This would indicate to me the injury occurred away from the pool." Patrick answered.

"That's right, I'd forgotten you're a former Chicago cop!"

"Also, please note, the body is wearing a housecoat which leads me to surmise she's either a resident or guest, and the assailant, also, is a resident or guest known to the victim." Patrick observed.

"Gads, you learn all that without touching the body! The police and the coroner are here now," the concierge announced, "I guess all they have to do is 'tie up the loose ends."

"Yeah! Like who, what, where and when. Piece of cake, huh?"

The crime scene investigators began photographing every angle around the pool, and, when finished, the coroner directed the removal of the corpse from the water for closer examination.

"From the condition of the body," He proclaimed, "I'd say this took place somewhere around three A.M."

The concierge informed the investigators that no outsiders had been logged into the building after eleven P.M., therefore she must have been an 'overnighter'

The police homicide Sergeant and his men began a floor-to-floor, apartment-to-apartment sweep, questioning everyone extensively, seeking any clues the residents might be able to provide.

The concierge identified the victim as Mrs. Rita Colismo an elderly widow from apartment 502 South. Also visiting in the condo were the niece of Mrs. 'C' and the niece's husband. They immediately became 'persons of interest'

Patrick logged onto his computer internet to assist the CSI team, with their approval, in back-grounding the young couple. The neice checked out OK, but the husband NOT so OK. He had a two-page 'rap sheet' of DUI's and petty violations of assaults and drunk and disorderly run-ins with the Buffalo, New York, police.

The two had solid alibis, however in that they had been spending their evening hitting the clubs along South Beach with two other couples. They did not return to the condo 'til after four AM, Long after the assault on Mrs. Colismo.

As soon as a search warrant was obtained, the CSI began a meticulous scouring of the vic's apartment. It turned up no clues so the investigators moved on to other possibilities.

What they did uncover was a new suspect.

The interrogation of other condo residents, revealed the victim was involved with 'Mr. Grouch' in 403 North.

It had been kept pretty hush-hush but two or three condo residents had observed a bit of 'touchy-feely' between the two on several occasions.

This information led Pat to go to his computer for another back ground screening on 'Mr. Grouch'.

Here pat's findings led to a further mystery There was NO record of the man before his arrival in Miami four years ago! No driver's license, No employment record, No Social Security records, and, No evidence that he ever existed!!

"I'd say we've found a prime suspect in this case, Sergeant," Pat suggested to the CSI detective, "I'm going to dig into the fingerprint files and see if we can find out who this bird **really is!**"

"I'd sure like to hear what you find out, detective," the police investigator voiced his curiosity, "We have here a probable felon wanted for something he did before he showed up here in Miami, which makes him the number one pigeon for **this** crime!"

When this new suspect took his trash to the dumpster, Patrick was right there, pawing through it for anything that might provide s fingerprint to run through his computer.

An empty soda can contained the answer.

The elaborate fingerprint data-base that Andy had programmed into his computer made quick work of identifying who our 'mystery man' really was He was an escaped prisoner from a Montana jail who had been doing fifty years for **murder** in a failed Bank holdup!

"Gottcha! Cowboy!" Pat addressed the computer screen.

"We'd best get the cuffs on this guy before he heads for 'high-country' again and crawls into anther 'rat-hole'!" the Miami detective exclaimed.

The arresting officers were almost too late taking down the fugitive. He had his bag all packed and was walking out the door when they grabbed him.

"Detective Ireland, I don't know how to thank you enough for your assistance. The Commissioner wants to see you and Sandy tomorrow. He didn't say why, but I guess it's to say 'thank you', also."

As it turned out that was not all he wanted to say.

"Detective Ireland, you and **PI, inc**. have the gratitude of our department and the City for the valuable assistance you rendered in bring that fugitive and murderer to justice.

"When we interrogated him he 'fessed up', but said the death of Mrs. Colismo was an accident. She had learned the truth about his past and a fight ensued. He gave her a violent shove to keep her from stopping him from leaving and she fell, hitting her head on the corner of a marble-topped coffee table.

"He cleaned up his apartment as well as he could. then carried her body up to the roof-top pool thinking no one would find her there until later in the morning, giving him a couple hours lead to make his get-away.

"He just didn't take into account that he was dealing with **PI, inc,** as well as the Miami cops.!"

That was not all the Commissioner had for Pat.

"Detective Ireland, the Mayor and I think it's only fitting that we swear you and your partner in as Auxiliary Police Officers with full powers to act in enforcing the laws of the City, the County, and the State of Florida. Hold up your right hand."

With the swearing in finished, Patrick retired to his apartment to file his report for the Police records, after which, with breakfast (coffee and a plate of Danish) in hand, he parked his frame on his balcony to let the Miami sun bake the fatigue from his bones.

FIFTEEN

It took two or three weeks for the dust to settle and life in the condominium to get back to normal for Detective Ireland.

Sandy was kept busy at the agency with the many requests for background checks and divorce actions, while Pat returned to the routine of riding the hallways on his scooter and visiting with the residents.

"Pat, ole Buddy," Ian commented, on one of his frequent visits on Pat's beach-watching balcony,

"I've just been offered four tickets for a seven-day Caribbean cruise. Why don't you and Sandy join me and the missus for a little jaunt on the 'bounding main'? I hear it's a sure cure for boredom and get's the old juices flowin' again."

"Sounds great to me, but Sandy has a new boy-friend and I don't think she'd go for it," Pat replied, "However, there's one of the single residents here who's been giving me the 'come-on' who I'm sure would jump at the proposition!"

"Fine, then, You make the offer to your condo-lady and I'll start making the arrangements for a sailing date."

Shipboard life was just what all four needed good food, entertainment, dancing, and lazy-ing in the deck chairs sipping Margaritas and Mai-tais, and soaking up the sea air and sunshine.

"This is just what the doctor ordered," Sally said, "Pat, how are you doing with your lady friend? She seems smitten, Anything cooking in the future"

"Nothing terribly romantic, Were playing it pretty platonic for now. Neither of us are 'in the market' for a steady relationship. She's a divorcee of three years and has settled into the single life. With a good sense of humor she is fun to be with. We have similar likes and dislikes, but we aren't looking for a permanent 'hook-up' any time soon. Who knows what the future might bring, though?" Patrick replied.

All too soon the cruise drew to an end and the four returned to their normal routines.

Pat called Sandy on his return:

"Sandy, you missed out on a great adventure," Pat informed her, "You need to go on one of these trips. You and your friend will feel rejuvenated after a sea-cruise, I guarantee it!"

"Sounds like a 'plan', to me," Sandy answered, *"meanwhile, during your adventure, life goes on at* **PI, inc.** *I've been kept hopping trying to keep up with all the background checks and cheating spouse cases. Right now we have three back-logged cases on which I could sure use a little help!"*

"OK, Girl, I'll be back in the office in the morning ready to tear into those files. See ya' then."

Patrick took over the two 'cheater' files and began his surveillance of the first one.

He parked his Spy mobile on a nearby street and began the watch.

This case involved a housewife who 'entertained' an A/C repairman all too regularly. I would appear her 'conditioning' needed more than normal 'adjusting'!

"Well, little lady, it appears 'Hubby' was right in his suspicions." Pat mused to himself. *"A few photos ought to wrap up this one in a 'flash!"* he chuckled.

"One down and one to go.!"

Sandy busied herself with the computer background search of one of the on-line lotharios and Pat picked up on the second straying spouse case. this one an office manager playing 'footsie' with the company bookkeeper.

Patrick observed several innocent lunches, covering them with photos, but still nothing incriminating. Five more days of surveillance, and still nothing.

Then, on the sixth afternoon, he followed the manager to a motel a couple miles away and, sure enough, shortly the bookkeeper drove up and the two proceeded to a room at the far end of the motel, All of this was duly recorded by Pat's lens.

Giving the couple a few minutes to 'get comfortable', Pat quietly made his way down the row of rooms. Pausing at the room the two had entered, he noted a small gap in the blinds through which he was able, with his tiny camera, to get pictures of the 'activity' within!

"That's two!" Patrick ticked off on his fingers.

Back at the office, Patrick filled out his report and called his two clients to inform them of the results with a full disclosure of evidence uncovered in his investigation Pat's security duties were a snap and left him with plenty of 'laid back' time. Most of the residents didn't have a need for his services. Maintenance took care of most of their minor problems.

For the most part, the condo residents preferred to just fire the culprit and claim it on their insurance. It simplified Patrick's responsibilities to just investigating and reporting.

Abe Jewell, the occupant of apartment 302 North, contacted Patrick with a request for his investigating services. He had signed a contract for a remodeling job on his kitchen. This would involve sub-contracting the replacing of wiring and plumbing.

The work was shoddy and only half complete when the contractor failed to pay the subs and they walked off the job.

"I want my money back or else satisfactory completion of the work," Abe told Pat.

"I agree, you're being taken for a ride by these contractors." Pat said, "I'll run a financial on all concerned and a BBB report. A lawyer will be able to use that info in court, if you decide to sue. A threat of a suit will probably convince those contractors to the negotiate or complete the work, for fear of losing their licenses.

"Don't worry about my fee, Abe. I'll just tack that on the settlement.," Patrick assured the tenant, "Keep me informed of any feedback you get from those contractors. If they drag their feet I have other pressures I can put in play all legal, of course!"

"My friends told me I could count on you. Thanks."

Patrick's investigation turned up several problems with the contractors. None of them had a credit rating above 500, and the BBB graded them all at 'C' or below. All-in-all poor risks!

"Abe," Pat informed his client, "I think you can kiss what money you've already soaked into your remodeling project 'good bye'! If you want to try suing them you have a good case,. However collecting anything is not likely!

"These kind of scammers always have a 'cut-and-run' plan in place in case they get nailed with a judgment against them. In most instances they just disappear and collecting is impossible. I've handled many such cases and all the client ever gets is **my bill** More wasted money!"

"Then you recommend not pursuing the matter?" Abe asked.

"Right! Unless you just enjoy 'the chase' and have money to throw down the drain," Pat replied.

"The 'chase' can get expensive and the results NADA! I can find the hole he's crawled into in a couple days, but then, it's weeks of 24/7 surveillance and legal wrangling court filings, etc. These guys just laugh it off and move on to their next 'mark'!" Pat reflected, "SAVE YOUR MONEY!"

"I appreciate your advice, Detective. Most private investigators would just keep the ball rolling and collecting fees with no results." Abe said.

"Abe, I don't operate that way. If I can't help my client, I tell him so and close the file!"

A new file was opened the next morning Someone on the inside was siphoning off products from one of Miami's better department stores and the management's own security staff were having no luck in uncovering the thieves.

When new items were ordered, the inventory that went on the shelves frequently didn't match the invoices.

Surveillance cameras throughout the store and warehouse were ineffective deterrents.

"We finally decided to put it in the hands of outside investigators," the store's CEO told Sandy during their initial phone contact. "**PI, inc.** came highly recommended by Miami/Dade Police, so we're putting the case in your hands."

"I want to set up a face-to-face with your head of security," Sandy told the exec. "Have him drop into our office tomorrow with all the information he and his staff have gathered to date. We'll run it through our computer and set up a data base to get things underway."

"I'll have the records in your office before noon," he assured her.

When Sandy began entering the info into the computer, it was immediately obvious that the majority of the thefts were in the small appliances, the electronics, and the jewelry department.

"All items easily concealed in small parcels, "Sandy noted.

Sandy called Pat and apprised him of this new case:

"I'm thinking' a putting three or four 'Secret Shoppers' in the store to closely monitor stock turn-over and to observe the movements of the employees might be our best approach. What do you think, Boss?"

"Hey! It's your show, Detective," Patrick said,

"Pat, I'd really like to have you in on this one. if you can breakaway from your balcony perch for a few days."

"Sure, Count me in. I need a cure for the boredom of 'bikini watchin' and wine-sipping with Ian. I'll be over with the Spy Mobile right after lunch!"

Sandy called in the aid of three off-duty female police to assist in 'secret shopping' and soon had a list of four low-level clerks with 'sticky fingers'. Background checks revealed this was not the first store they'd 'heisted'.

With the evidence gathered, the thieves were soon hauled off to the lock-up.

"That catches us up so I'm back to bein' a 'House Dick' and lounging on my balcony," Pat announced to Sandy, "keep in touch and call if you need me again. I'm always available."

Ian and Pat were back on the balcony sippin' and snackin' and watchhing the sun bake the oiled-up bods lying on the white sand.

"Now this is what I call **Retierment** with a capital '**R**'." Patrick pronounced with a chuckle.

"Yeah, Pal, it don't get much more '**Retired**' than this!"

* * *